The City of the Golden Sun

Sequel to The Fisherman's Son

by

Marilyn Peake

This book is a work of fiction. Places, events, and situations in this story are purely fictional. Any resemblance to actual persons, living or dead, is coincidental.

First published by AuthorHouse 04/21/04

ISBN: 1-4184-1057-8 (Paperback)

This book is printed on acid free paper.

To Billy and Benny who light up every day, and fill every day with happiness. Thank you for your wonderful enthusiasm.

And to Bill – Thank you for your support, for your computer expertise, and for all of the joy you've brought into my life.

Part I

On Land, in Wiley's Village

Early 1800's

CHAPTER 1

Wiley O'Mara woke with a start. At first he wasn't sure where he was. He had the distinct impression that he had experienced an incredible dream. Then the memories came rushing in. He and the six children from the city at the bottom of the ocean had made it to land and fallen asleep in Wiley's tree house.

He rubbed his eyes, blinked and looked around. They were all there. Keegan, the son of an ancient King, whose name meant "little and fiery." Keegan was fast asleep on the wooden floor, his head resting on his right arm, breathing rhythmically in and out, slowly and peacefully. His long, golden hair fell across his arm and spilled onto the floor. It sparkled with bits of sunshine that danced into the tree house through the narrow openings in each set of shutters.

Three other boys were asleep at the wooden table, their heads resting on their folded arms. The oldest was Arthur Bragon. He was twelve years old, tall, muscular and strong. He had dark black hair down to his shoulders, intense blue eyes and thick, dark eyebrows. He was intelligent, a serious thinker, and athletic. His parents had had big dreams and aspirations for him. They had thought that perhaps he would one day grow up to be a Senator.

The next oldest boy was Calder Torannen. He was eleven years old and Arthur's best friend. He had red hair, pale skin splashed generously with freckles, and a mercurial disposition. His great passion in life was to one day become an actor in the city theater.

The youngest boy at the table was Nevin Quigley. He was ten years old, an acquaintance who sometimes spent time with Arthur and Calder. He was thin and short for his age. He had light brown hair, green eyes, and a winning personality. His primary talents involved making people laugh and pulling practical jokes. Arthur and Calder enjoyed the humor that Nevin added to their free time.

Another boy had fallen asleep on the wooden chest that Wiley's father had built. Wiley thought he looked very uncomfortable, resting on the hard surface. This was Neil Quigley, the youngest of all the boys. He was Nevin's younger brother, six years old. He was gentle and easygoing in nature, sensitive, affectionate and quick to laugh. He had soft, golden curls for hair, hazel eyes, a small nose and delicate lips. Like his brother, Nevin, he was thin and short for his age.

During the night, Neil had pulled his knees up against his chest and wrapped his arms around them for warmth and comfort. He slept so deeply, Wiley could barely tell that he was breathing. A nearly imperceptible rise and fall in the upper part of his back let Wiley know that Neil was still with them.

The last boy in the group was Kingston Ivers. He was twelve years old, an acquaintance of Keegan who happened to be in the library at the time when the meteor hit the ancient city. He was tall and muscular with a strong, outspoken personality. He had dark brown hair, deep brown eyes and ruddy cheeks. If you disagreed with him on things that mattered to him, he could be difficult.

Kingston was asleep on the floor, wrapped in a blanket he had found in the tree house.

Wiley had also slept on the floor, wrapped in a dark gray, woolen blanket from deep inside the wooden chest. He sat up and wrapped the cover more tightly about him. It was early morning. The air still held a chill, although the sun's rays had started entering the tree house through the openings between the window shutters.

Wiley let the warmth from the blanket seep into his bones. As he looked around the room at each individual sleeping boy, he wondered how he would introduce the boys to his island or to his century. His island, their island, was no longer the same as when the boys had lived their lives here. No one would be familiar to them. Everyone they had known, except for each other, had died a long time ago. Their city was under the ocean. The island was now impoverished, and the boys had known great wealth. Keegan was the son of a King.

Wiley remembered his journey through the forest to find a priest to bury his mother. He had thought that he could not make that journey either. But, once he had decided to put one foot in front of the other and keep on going, the universe had opened up to him, and he had succeeded.

And incredible things had happened after that. Elden, the dolphin, had led him to Keegan and five other boys in a lost city under the ocean. He had fought the Fire Beast and rescued the boys!

Now Wiley wondered what to do. Probably I should just put one foot in front of the other, do what needs to be done one thing at a time, and the universe will reveal the future step-by-step.

The first thing to do, Wiley realized, was to find out if his father was at home. It was not yet time for his father to meet the boys. The boys should probably be introduced to someone else first, maybe Mrs. Bannon.

Wiley pondered whether to leave the boys now while they were sleeping and go investigate his house, or wait for them to wake up. He was afraid to have the boys wake up without him. He wasn't sure what they would do, or if they would leave the tree house and go out into the village alone. He worried about what they might tell the villagers. You couldn't exactly say you were from a city that sank to the bottom of the ocean thousands of years ago. You couldn't exactly say you were rescued by Wiley on the back of a dolphin. The villagers did not respond well to foreigners or to people who were different. They would label the boys insane, and that did not bode well for their stay on the island. Or for Wiley's future.

Wiley decided that he would make a quick run to his house to see if his father was there and if there was food in the cupboards. As he opened the tree house door, the sunlight poured in like a flood. It washed over Neil Quigley as he slept on the wooden chest and seeped behind his closed eyelids. Neil awoke with a start and let out a wail. As he screamed and cried, Wiley became increasingly concerned that someone would hear him, and that he would not be able to control the young boy.

Neil's screams woke the other boys. Nevin, his older brother, let out a scream before he knew what had awakened him. The other boys rubbed their eyes and looked around the tree house. Nevin composed himself, walked over to Neil, sat on the wooden chest, and wrapped his arms around his younger brother.

"Shhh, Neil. Shhh. You can't scream like that, Neil. You're going to get us in a lot of trouble. Do you want to get locked up in jail or something?"

Nevin looked at Wiley, as if to ask, "Could that actually happen?" Wiley looked at Nevin and shrugged his shoulders.

Neil continued to cry and scream. Wiley looked at Nevin. "He's hysterical. We're going to get caught!"

Nevin stood in front of Neil and grabbed him by the shoulders. He bent down, looked him in the face, and said with great desperation, "Neil, stop it! You're going to get us all caught, and we're not going to be treated well! I mean it! Stop it!"

Realizing that his older brother was scared, Neil quieted his voice but continued sobbing into his blanket.

Nevin looked at Wiley. "At least he's quiet. That should be acceptable."

"That's fine. I'm wondering what we should do next. I thought we should find some food. Sometimes my father is at home, sometimes he's not. My father is very …" Wiley paused briefly, "difficult."

Keegan looked at Wiley. "What about your mother?"

Wiley looked at the ground. "My mother died. Shortly before I found you. I'll tell you about that later."

"I'm sorry."

Wiley shuffled his feet and wiped a small tear from his right eye. "Well, we need to decide what to do. My father can't see you. He drinks. Sometimes he's violent. There's a woman on the island, Mrs. Bannon. She took care of me after my mother died. She's very kind, she makes good food, and she's generous."

Arthur Bragon spoke up, "That sounds like a plan. I'm starving! What do we do … just go to her house?"

Wiley looked at the six boys. He suddenly realized something. "No. We can't just show up there. People in my village know everyone else in the village. You can't just show up. We have to make up a story about where you all came from. Maybe the story that Elden suggested: that you were all shipwrecked. But there's another problem …" Wiley paused and looked at each of the six boys. "Look at the way you're dressed."

Kingston Ivers looked from one boy to the other. "What do you mean, look at the way we're dressed?" Kingston's face turned red. He clenched his right fist repeatedly, looking Wiley directly in the eye.

"Well, you're wearing tunics."

"So? What do you mean by that? Everyone wears tunics!"

Wiley looked again at all six boys. Keegan wore an oatmeal colored tunic, a kind of a dress, that fell halfway down his calf. He wore an oatmeal colored toga over the tunic. To Wiley, the toga looked like a fancy blanket that Keegan had draped over his left shoulder, then wrapped around himself by going under his opposite arm and tucking it into the front. The toga was trimmed in purple and gold stripes and looked very regal. Keegan wore brown sandals trimmed in gold.

Arthur wore only a tunic and sandals. His tunic was made from gray wool and was tied at the waist with a dark brown belt. His sandals were made from brown leather.

Calder wore a wrinkled, light brown tunic with no belt and no shoes.

Nevin's tunic was light tan in color and also very wrinkled. Like Calder, he was not wearing shoes.

Neil Quigley wore a tunic the same oatmeal color as Keegan's, and a toga identical to Keegan's except that it was trimmed in bright red stripes. He wore red shoes that resembled slippers or some type of closed sandals.

Kingston Ivers who presently seemed furious at Wiley wore a tan tunic tied at the waist with a brown belt and brown leather sandals. Wiley did not like the way a muscle kept rising and falling in Kingston's right arm as he clenched and unclenched his fist.

Wiley looked into Kingston's reddened face and glistening brown eyes. "Well, look at the way I'm dressed!"

Kingston looked briefly at Wiley's black pants and gray woolen shirt. "So?"

Wiley swallowed. "Don't you get it? You're from a different time period. Your city existed thousands of years ago. If you show up dressed like that, out of nowhere, don't you think people in my village will get suspicious?"

Kingston relaxed his hand and stopped clenching his fist. He paced across the tree house floor. His brown leather sandals padded swiftly back and forth across the hard wooden surface, making sounds like a cat pondering its next move.

Kingston stopped, turned quickly around, and looked at Wiley. "I've got it! You're right … We should tell everyone we've been shipwrecked. Do you have blankets, or clothes that will fit us? Any of us who can fit into your clothes will wear them. Any of us who can't fit into your clothes will wrap blankets around us, like we lost our clothes in the shipwreck."

Wiley looked at Kingston and admired his quick thinking. "That works! My family always has blankets. In winter, it's very cold on this island."

Neil's hazel eyes widened as he stared at Kingston and Wiley. He felt proud that Kingston who was from his city and his time period had solved the problem. But he felt frightened and very much alone. He wanted his mother. Where was his mother?

CHAPTER 2

Wiley left the boys in the tree house and quietly approached his home. He walked carefully through the deep emerald grass, feeling the cool morning dew wash over his bare feet. He noticed again the beauty of the flowers he had planted with his father. Throughout the yard, wherever Wiley's father had cleared out patches of ground, there rose splashes of red, purple, pink and yellow petals. They exploded outward from deep green stalks and leaves. Wiley noticed dew dripping down the colorful petals and green leaves and collecting in the yellow, powdery centers of flowers. A sweet perfume floated on the air.

Wiley wanted to pause and take in the yard, but he realized that he needed to hurry. He resumed his quick, quiet approach to his home.

Wiley looked at his house as he crossed the yard. It looked small and plain, cold and hard. Made from gray and white rocks fitted tightly together, it was an adequate shelter. It had seemed warmer, and somehow larger, when Wiley's mother had been alive. She had filled the home with laughter and love, with the sweet smell of baking bread, the noise of cooking pans and bubbling stews. She often sang while she worked, filling the home with ballads and hymns. In the evening, Wiley's mother had told stories as she knitted by the fire. Her favorite stories were folk legends and those about the island.

Wiley remembered when she had first told him about The Beast in the Forest. She had told him that a huge beast with three glowing eyes and large fangs inhabited the forest next to their home. She had told him that it could stand on its hind legs like a bear, or drop on all fours and run as fast as a wolf. She had told him never to enter the forest because the Beast ran faster than young children, and that he would never be able to escape.

And yet, at twelve years of age, Wiley had outwitted and escaped the Beast. Perhaps he was no longer a child, a fact of life and a fear that had begun slowly to take root in his conscious mind.

Wiley looked at the stone chimney. No smoke, so no one was cooking. Wiley hoped that his father would not be home. So far, so good.

When Wiley reached the massive, dark brown, wooden front door to his home, he paused and stared, as if waiting for the door to speak. To tell him whether or not it would be safe on the other side. To tell him whether or not all would be safe and good beyond this point in time.

Wiley shivered from the cold, liquid dew evaporating from his feet. He slowly turned the black metal doorknob to his home, pushed open the door and stepped inside.

The deep quiet rushed toward the opening and surrounded him like a warm, thick blanket. It muffled the outdoor sounds, and filled the house with a pervading sense of absence. His father wasn't home!

He had to move quickly.

Wiley ran to the fireplace to see if there were hot ashes. Nothing. The ashes were cold. That meant that his father had not cooked recently. Probably he had been away. Which meant that he might stay away, or that he might return any minute. A shiver ran down Wiley's spine.

He turned and walked over to the large, dark, wooden trunk next to the fireplace. He paused and stared at the portrait of fishing boats carved into the lid. The boats were at sea, riding the powerful waves of the ocean. The porous wood of the trunk had absorbed the smell of his father's spilt whiskey.

Memories flooded into Wiley's conscious mind and removed him from his present situation into the past. They were a mixture of pleasure and pain. He remembered fishing with his father, going out on a large vessel into the sea. He remembered the patience of the men as they waited to make their catch. The water rising up in huge walls of salty spray and splashing onto the deck. He remembered the calm, serene days when the depth of the ocean revealed itself in the heavy, thick movement of deep blue water against the sides of the boat. Wiley remembered looking over the boat railing, gazing into the impenetrable depth of blue liquid. He remembered seeing nothing beyond the surface, wondering how far down to the bottom, when suddenly a fish would fly up from the depths and show itself in the sunlit air. He remembered the brilliant flash of silver or gold before the fish returned to the sea.

Wiley remembered the songs of the fishermen, the occasional songs of humpback whales, and the cries of gulls close to shore. He remembered the crusty layer of salt that accumulated on his skin after days at sea, the way it tugged at his skin and made him ache for home.

And he remembered the whiskey scent of his father that always, eventually, brought happiness to a close. He remembered the screaming and the violence. He remembered his mother, her endless patience.

Well, no time to think about all of that now. He had to hurry. Wiley lifted the heavy wooden lid, turning the boats upside down, and looked inside. "Thank you, God!" Wiley looked toward the ceiling. "Thank you, Mother!" He had lately the feeling that his mother was watching over him, even after her death. There, in the deep recesses of the wooden chest, were three heavy fleece blankets: one gray, one white, one a mixture of both. They looked new! A neighbor must have delivered them to Wiley's father. Oh, how they would come in handy!

Wiley reached in and grabbed the three blankets. He then ran into the kitchen, dumped them temporarily on the kitchen table and yanked open the doors to all of the kitchen cabinets. There was food! Who had done this?

Wiley stared, trying to take in the realization that there was more food than he could carry. Then he shook the fog from his brain and concentrated. He pushed all but the gray blanket onto the floor. He opened the gray blanket so that it covered the table, and started piling food onto its open surface.

Wiley chose both things that would sustain him and things that would delight him. He filled the blanket with jars of strawberry, raspberry and blueberry jam, potatoes, wheels of cheese, homemade breads, two homemade cakes, and several jars of honey. Then he realized: This won't work. The heavy things will crush the soft things.

Wiley quickly emptied the gray blanket, brushed it onto the floor; then filled it with the heavy items, such as the jars of jam and honey and the wheels of cheese. He threw the white blanket on top of the items in order to protect them, gathered the edges of the gray blanket together and tied them into a large knot. Likewise, after placing the softer items within, Wiley gathered up the edges of the gray-and-white blanket and worked them into a knot. Then he picked up the two large bundles, and slipped one over each shoulder.

As he turned the doorknob on his front door and left his home, Wiley felt as though he had done something wrong. But he hadn't. The lives of six other boys now depended on him.

Once outside, Wiley breathed the morning air deeply into his lungs. He felt his chest swell from the sudden inhalation. The sweet smell of flowers mingled with the salty scent of the sea. Wiley marveled at the deep green of the moist grass, and the splashes of color arising from every place that he and his father had planted seeds in a time that seemed so long ago.

Wiley stepped into the grass, carrying his sacks of food. Then, suddenly, he turned and bolted back into the house. He placed his bundles on the floor by the front door and ran over to his bed. He threw back the top blanket. He saw nothing but the mattress. He tore the blanket off the bed, then the pillow. He held his head for a moment and stared at the ceiling, as though praying for memory. He went over to the storage chest and flung back the lid with all of its carved fishing boats. The chest was empty. He looked in the fireplace, as though he might see what he was looking for among the ashes. Then he looked under his bed. There it was! A cloth doll that a ncighbor had made for him many years ago. It was very simple: tan cloth with painted brown eyes, a spattering of brown freckles, and thin lips painted a light shade of red. Brown lines had been drawn on the top of its head to represent hair; and clothes had been painted right onto the body. The doll that had been made to look like Wiley had also been designed to forever wear a gray, long-sleeve shirt with brown pants. The feet had been left bare, still showing the original tan cloth.

Wiley snatched up the doll from under his bed; then ran quickly to a wooden crate in the corner of the room. He pulled three pairs of pants and three shirts from the container. Realizing that he would be offering his clothes to boys from the wealthy city under the ocean, he suddenly realized that his clothes were full of patches and holes. Most of them had belonged to older children in the neighborhood, or had been sewn together from scraps of material by his mother. He had one pair of pants that were blue on one side and green on the other. He saw them in the crate, but wouldn't even consider offering them to his new friends. Neighbors were used to seeing Wiley dress that way; but he didn't want the boys to stand out for their clothing.

After gathering the other pants and shirts together, Wiley ran to the bundles near the front door and squeezed the clothing into the gray blanket. Then he ran into the kitchen and threw open a cupboard door. He took down a metal container. Opening the lid, he saw the treasure that he had suddenly hoped would be there. Hard, sticky candy balls that would taste like strawberry and sugar. He put the lid back on the container and ran for the front door.

When Wiley reached the bundles, he hoisted one over each shoulder. He tucked the metal container under his right arm and clasped the doll tightly with his right hand. Then he opened the door, stepped outside, turned quickly around, and shut the front door.

Wiley walked as quickly as he could without damaging the food he was carrying, across the yard, over to the tree house. When he reached the bottom of the tree house stairs, he put his fingers in his mouth and whistled.

The door opened a crack. Arthur Bragon peeked out.

"Come on! This stuff is heavy!" Wiley looked up the long wooden ladder to where Arthur stood looking at him.

As soon as he realized who was at the base of the tree, Arthur swung the door wide open. Five other faces quickly filled the space, as Arthur climbed down to help Wiley.

"Here, give me one of those sacks!"

Wiley handed Arthur the lighter one first. "Be careful! There's food in there that's fragile!" Wiley looked at Neil and lowered his voice, " … cakes and stuff."

Neil's eyes grew wide. He started running around the tree house in anticipation.

Arthur gently threw the sack over his back and climbed up into the tree house. He placed the sack made from the gray-and-white blanket on the wooden table and quickly looked at all the boys. "Now, no one touch this until I get back!" Arthur looked at Neil who seemed oblivious to his warning. "Neil, that includes you!" When Neil looked at him blankly, Arthur realized that he hadn't heard a word. "Neil, do not touch this package until I get back!"

Neil's eyes quickly filled with tears. He stopped running around. "I won't."

Arthur felt badly that he had yelled at Neil; but he figured that he would make it up to him when he showed him the food. If Wiley had found something that Neil would especially like, Arthur would allow him to have it.

Arthur went back down the ladder.

"Here, Arthur, can you take this? It's very heavy."

"Sure." Arthur answered automatically, before he had tested the entire weight of the gray blanket. He almost dropped it; it was surprisingly heavy. Glass containers clanked together.

"No! Arthur, be careful!"

"I'm sorry! This is incredible! What's in here?"

"You'll see."

Wiley waited until Arthur was safely up the ladder and in the tree house, so that there was no chance of getting hit by a falling jar of jam or the entire lot within the blanket. Then Wiley went up the ladder with the metal container of sweets under his right arm, and the doll swinging from his right hand.

When Wiley entered the house, he found all the boys gathered around the blanket packages on the wooden table. He gave his permission for Arthur and Keegan to open them. With his tears completely dried and forgotten, Neil started jumping up and down.

Keegan opened the gray-and-white blanket first. There was a gasp from all the boys, and then happy shouting from Neil.

"Can I have a piece of cake? Please! Please, Nevin? Please!"

Nevin gave his permission, and then ripped away a piece of cake with his bare hands. Neil gobbled it up in seconds, and then asked for more.

"Wait, Neil, everyone should have a piece."

Neil started to cry.

Wiley moved to the front of the small crowd and leaned against the table. He slowly opened the gray blanket. After undoing the large knot but before revealing the contents, he spoke to the boys. "I want you to know that I found a great deal of food in my house. But that situation is rare. I come from a very poor family. Since my mother died, some of our neighbors have been very kind and helpful. My guess is that someone stopped by recently and left food. All of our neighbors are poor. This will probably not happen again for a long, long time. I will show you all of the food I found; but we need to ration it and save much of it for later."

Looking at the glistening excitement in their eyes, Wiley opened the gray blanket. There was a gasp more pronounced than the first one, and then utter quiet. The silence was broken by Neil.

"Please, please, Nevin! Get me some jam?"

Wiley moved the small pile of clothing within the blanket onto a chair. Then he reached over and grabbed a jar of strawberry jam. He opened the jar, grabbed a loaf of bread, ripped off a huge chunk, and sank the bread into the thick, red gel.

"Here, Neil, you'll like this. The jam is very sweet."

The boys, under the watchful eye of Wiley, carefully made their selections. Arthur decided to have bread and cheese for strength, with a very small taste of cake. Keegan chose bread dipped in honey and a large piece of cheese. For reasons that no one else could understand, Nevin grabbed a chunk of cheese, dipped it in strawberry jam, and added a small piece of bread on the side. Calder picked cheese and a piece of homemade cake. Kingston chose a combination that Neil later wished he had thought of: homemade cake slathered with strawberry jam.

When the boys were finished with their first tree house meal, one jar of strawberry jam was completely empty. Neil ran his fingers around the sweetened inside of the glass container and licked them clean, until it seemed impossible that anything had ever filled the jar.

Wiley gently took the container from Neil's hand. "I think that's enough, Neil. Let me take that."

Wiley then walked over to the wooden seat built into one side of the tree house and lifted it up. "Look, everyone. I'm going to put the food into this storage compartment, so that no one will find it while we're gone. Because we have a limited amount of food, if anyone wants to eat anything, they have to get the approval of everyone else. Got it?"

All the boys except Neil shook their head in agreement. Neil drew his eyebrows up into small arches and looked worried.

With the help of Arthur and Kingston, Wiley moved all of the food from the table into the storage compartment. Then he opened a set of windows and shook the blankets out, so that all of the loose crumbs fell to the ground.

Then he spoke to the boys, "All right. Now it's time to get dressed."

Wiley looked at the boys, sizing them up. "Calder, Nevin, and Keegan, I think you can wear my clothes. I think they'll fit you. Kingston, Arthur, and Neil, I think you'll have to do the blanket trick. You know, wrap a blanket around you and say that you lost your clothes in a shipwreck."

Calder spoke up. "I have another idea. Why don't we wear our own clothes, and say that we're wearing costumes for a play?"

Wiley remembered how, in the village on the other side of the forest, there were people with enough food to give piecrust to chickens. He also remembered, somewhat sadly, how he had eaten some of that piecrust off the ground. He remembered the taste of dirt mixed with the piecrust and how delicious the crust had tasted all the same.

Then the answer came to him, how he would hide the boys.

"I've got it!"

The boys stared at Wiley as though he had gone mad.

"I'm sorry. Not about the clothes. We don't have plays here. The most we have are small Church plays, and there's never enough money for costumes. We just wear our own clothes. But I've got it about where you can live! There's an orphanage on the other side of the forest."

"An orphanage? But we've got a home!" Kingston looked indignant. A thick vein in his forehead started to pulse.

"Well, right now, you don't." Wiley looked at Neil, in order to gauge the impact of his words. Neil was looking away, playing with a small pile of sticks that Wiley had accidentally dragged into the tree house with the blankets. "Here's what I think we should do. Get dressed in my clothes and blankets, not in your clothes, in case my neighbors see you. Then we sneak away from my village through the forest next to my house. On the other side of the forest is another village. Most people over there don't know me. But there's an orphanage where people do know me." Wiley paused briefly. "We should go there. They'll feed you and take care of you. I'll go down to the ocean and try to speak with Elden, the dolphin who protected you and led me to find you. I'll ask him what we should do next."

Kingston was about to say something, when Wiley interrupted him. "Oh, one more thing. The forest has magic in it." A stillness pervaded the tree house. Everyone stared at Wiley. "It's a good kind of magic. It helped me during a very difficult time in my life - right after my mother died, when I needed to pass through the forest to find a priest in the other village to bury my mother."

The boys from the city under the ocean were speechless, taking in the information that Wiley was telling them, waiting for him to continue.

"There's a magical woman in the forest named Lucinda. She appeared to me near an oval lake. The lake is very special. It has healing qualities. I once dove in with a huge gash in my arm; it healed immediately." Wiley looked at Neil. He decided to refrain from telling the boys that the gash had come from a ferocious bear. Although he had defeated the animal in battle, her cub had survived. Wiley wasn't sure how much the cub might have grown by now, or if it would remember him.

Wiley continued, "The lake water, mixed with special flowers from the forest, healed the dolphin Elden after he was attacked by the Fire Beast guarding your city." Wiley paused. "The lake will also show you visions. It's up to you to interpret them; but you'll probably see them."

Wiley suddenly remembered something, "And there is food in the forest. A rabbit led me to a patch of delicious, ripe, wild strawberries."

With his chin held high, Keegan looked directly into Wiley's eyes with the wisdom of someone much older than this future King. "Let's go. We'll do it. It sounds like our best chance."

Neil, who was sitting on thc floor, bent his knees up to his chin, tucked them tightly against his chest, and placed his head on folded arms. Then he started to cry.

Nevin who had been sitting next to Neil put his left arm around his younger brother. "What's wrong, Neil?"

"I'm scared."

"We're all scared."

At that point, Wiley went over to a corner of the tree house where he had hidden his doll and the tin of candy under an old rug. He picked up the items and brought them to Neil. "Neil, everything will turn out all right. You'll see. I thought you might like these."

The little boy looked up suspiciously. Then a ray of happiness lit up his face from within. His eyes widened as he reached for the doll and the tin. He hugged the doll tightly under one arm and carefully opened the container. It was as though the sun had suddenly broke free from the clouds.

"Can I have one?"

Wiley looked at Nevin as he responded, "I think that that would be all right. They're mostly for you."

CHAPTER 3

Wiley led the way into the forest. This time, six boys followed him. He remembered the first time that he had entered this darkened realm. He had been alone, and terrified of the myth about The Beast in the Forest. Now he had some concern, but not terror. He was worried about the bear cub. How much had it grown? Would it remember that he had killed its mother?

Wiley took comfort in the fact that Lucinda also inhabited this forest, and that she might come to his aid were he to find himself in trouble. Especially since he had the six boys from the ancient city under his protection.

As they entered the forest, it was as it had been before. It was quiet except for the sounds of birds somewhere in the trees. The forest seemed to keep an even temperature. Whereas it was warmer than the cold outside in winter, it was now cooler than the warmth of summer. It was refreshing and pleasant. Again, there was the soft carpet of pine needles underfoot, and the pungent smell of dirt and pine trees.

Neil passed by Wiley and ran ahead of the group. Wiley thought to call him back, but instead just yelled at him to stay in sight.

Neil, suddenly forgetting that he was lost in time with only five other survivors from a city that sank to the bottom of the ocean thousands of years ago, ran ahead down the forest path. Wiley envied him his carefree youth.

Neil cavorted down the path, singing and humming, and skipping at times. Once in awhile, he would bend down to look at something very carefully, a bug in the dirt or a flower blossoming under the trees. Once he bent to pick up a stick, and then proceeded along the path waving the stick as though brandishing a sword.

Suddenly, Neil stopped in his tracks. Wiley's heart pounded against his chest. His fingers trembled. He whispered as loudly as he could, "Everyone, get back! Neil, get over here, now!"

Then he saw what Neil saw. A family of white rabbits. A large rabbit, probably the mother, and three small bunnies. As Wiley had witnessed once before with only one rabbit, sunlight poured through the canopy and illuminated the rabbits.

"Neil, follow them. See where they lead you."

As before, the large rabbit led the way down the path to the wild strawberry patch. The bunnies followed their mother, jumping through the lush, red strawberries and overgrown vines. The mother kept a close eye on her little ones.

The boys were as delighted as Wiley had been the first time he had discovered the patch. They ripped strawberries from the vines and stuffed them into their faces as though they might never eat again. Neil had sweet, red, sticky juice running down his chin and covering his fingers. Wiley ate more carefully, but thoroughly enjoyed the delicious red fruit.

When the boys were done, the rabbits scampered off. Neil yelled after them; but Wiley warned him to be quiet.

"Come here. I want to show you something."

Wiley led the way through the forest to the place where the canopy opened to the sky. As before, the oval lake glistened in the sun, reflecting the pure white clouds moving overhead.

Keegan gasped. "That's incredible."

"Lucinda led me here. She's the magical woman who inhabits the forest." Wiley studied the boys to see how much of his story they would accept. "She gave me a golden cup from your city. One of the cups decorated with gemstones, engraved with the words: 'Drink deeply by land or sea. Earth comes only once.' She told me to take the cup down to the beach and show it to a dolphin. The dolphin was Elden. After I showed him the cup, he led me to all of you in your underwater city."

Wiley thought how simplified this version of the story sounded, in comparison to all that he had experienced.

Keegan's eyes opened wide. He stood silently frozen in the forest path. Wiley thought how regal he looked, standing with his hands on his hips, chin jutted forward, wearing a toga and tunic trimmed in purple and gold. The sun reflected off the gold on Keegan's sandals. Wiley was glad that Keegan and the boys who would wrap themselves in blankets had decided to save that for later, after their trek through the forest.

"Why are you looking at me like that, Keegan?"

"The golden cup. That belonged to a set of golden goblets owned by the royal family, my family."

"Well, Elden must have borrowed one to lead me to you."

"I suppose."

"Here, try this." Wiley walked down to the water's edge. "Lucinda gave me the golden cup to dip into the lake for a drink. But we can use our hands instead. The water has healing properties. You'll feel refreshed and invigorated."

Wiley knelt down in the muddy grass at the edge of the lake. He saw, once again, the tiny purple flowers that grew there. He smelled the mixture of mud and perfumed petals. He dipped his cupped hands into the water and drank deeply. His vision intensified; he felt renewed.

The boys followed Wiley's example.

Neil slurped the water noisily from his hands. Then, as suddenly as he had joined in the fun of imitating Wiley, he stopped. He was frozen in time as though turned to ice. Then he screamed. One long, low wail of a sound that carried pain and shock. Wiley ran over to Neil, then followed his gaze into the water.

Wiley saw nothing but the purple fish with black eyes. He smiled at the vision; but then thought better of the smile.

"Neil, what's the problem? What do you see?"

Neil extended his arm and pointed. He mumbled in a slow, hesitant voice, "My mother. My mother is in the lake. She's underwater. Why is this happening?"

The vision was true. Neil's mother was indeed underwater for all the rest of eternity. Did this mean that Wiley's earlier vision had had some truth in it? He had seen the face of a wolf that had changed into his own face, and then into a head with the face of his father on one side and the face of his mother on the other. What had Lucinda said to him? "This is your destiny. To bring the two halves together ... Destiny is bigger than what you can understand at the moment."

As he was about to turn away from the powerful memory and address Neil, he heard a voice. A pleasant, lyrical voice, a voice like no other he had ever heard. Except one.

"All of you have made it. Welcome."

Wiley looked up. Lucinda floated above the lake. Her golden hair fell to her waist. Her green eyes sparkled. In her right hand, she held her golden staff decorated with gemstones. She wore a pure white dress tied with blue ribbons at the waist. On her feet, she wore golden slippers decorated with the same gemstones as on her staff.

Lucinda floated closer to shore. She waved gently and slowly to Keegan. He did not answer, only stared at the vision in front of him. Lucinda reached into a deep pocket in her dress and pulled out a golden goblet, the same type that she had given to Wiley earlier.

"I believe this belongs to you."

Keegan did not respond.

"Here, take it. It's yours."

Lucinda waved the cup up-and-down until Keegan responded and took it.

Keegan turned the cup over and over in his hands, inspecting the gemstones, the tiny engraved dolphin on each side of the line of words, and the inscription that read, "Drink deeply by land or sea. Earth comes only once." This was indeed one of the goblets belonging to his royal family.

Lucinda again spoke to Keegan, "Does this cup not belong to you?"

Keegan answered hesitantly, "Yes, it's mine. It belongs to my family."

Lucinda looked at Wiley. "You have done well. You have begun to fulfill your destiny. Things are unfolding as they should. Go back to the ocean. Do not continue on. Do not go to the orphanage. You will need to go there later. For now, go back to the beach. Once again, show Elden the cup. Make sure that all of the boys are with you. Elden will know what to do."

As Wiley was about to answer, she disappeared. The boys looked at each other, to make sure that they had all seen and heard the same thing. They never spoke; but noticed a stunned look on each boy's face. They assumed that they had all seen the same thing.

CHAPTER 4

Wiley was the first to move. He walked away from the lakeshore through the long, green and muddied grass. A silver-blue fish broke the surface of the lake behind him, then splashed back into its watery world. The cool water closed in around the ripples and returned the lake to its mirrored surface.

Wiley crossed a stretch of thin, dry, yellow grass. Then he stepped onto the forest path. Suddenly, as though changing his mind, he turned quickly around and planted his shoes firmly in the dirt. The quick, circular movement sent small clouds of dust into the air, covering his ankles in smoke.

Wiley looked down the path in the direction of the lake. He saw Kingston Ivers standing there, arms crossed, with a solid body that looked both strong and tall. Wearing a tunic and brown leather sandals, Kingston displayed pronounced muscles in both his arms and calves.

He called to Wiley, “We’re not going in that direction!”

“What do you mean?”

“I mean, we’re going to the orphanage. You said there was food there, and a place to stay!”

“Yes; but that’s all changed now. You heard Lucinda!”

"Lucinda?"

"Yes." Wiley worried that perhaps Lucinda had existed only in his imagination and that the other boys might not have seen her.

"You mean, I'm supposed to listen to a little fairy woman floating in golden slippers above the lake? When there's food and a place to stay on the other side of the forest?"

The lake remained motionless. Like a blue porcelain bowl holding tufts of white wool, it reflected the clouds moving overhead. A large, black bird swooped down low over the lake, called to its brethren, and searched for fish. As it flapped its wings, the bird pushed the air forward, creating a whooshing noise above the water.

Small animals scurried through the underbrush. The trees that lined the far side of the lake stood like silent guardians of time. A strong breeze rolled across the lake and bent the canopy, creating the silvery music of whispering leaves.

"Lucinda is not a little fairy woman! You cannot disobey her! She knows what she's talking about!"

Arthur stepped in front of Kingston and faced him. "I think we should listen to Wiley. He knows this place better than we do."

"Oh, you think so? I don't care! I'm not going back to a tree house when I can stay in a real house with plenty of food!"

Arthur took another step toward Kingston until they were so close Kingston could smell his breath. At that point, Kingston took the flattened palm of his hand and shoved it hard into the other boy's chest. Arthur winced and instinctually stepped backward.

"Take that! Get out of my face, Arthur! I can go where I want!"

Arthur recovered and rushed toward Kingston. He tackled him, knocked him to the ground, and punched him in the face. The punch made a thudding sound that sickened Wiley.

Keegan puffed himself up and yelled loudly, "Stop it! Stop it!" The royal demand changed nothing. Kingston and Arthur, locked in battle, continued to scuffle on the ground.

Wiley, Calder, and Nevin charged the fighting boys and pried them apart. Arthur stomped off toward the lake. Kingston stood up and gently pressed the palm of his hand against his throbbing right cheek. A black-and-purple swelling had already erupted there, where Arthur had punched him.

Wiley looked Kingston directly in the eye and said matter-of-factly as though teaching him an important lesson, "Go down to the lake. Put water on it. It will heal the moment the water touches it."

"Yeah, right."

"Please, Kingston, just do it!"

Kingston walked to the lake, dragging his feet and slouching, in defiance of the poor boy giving him orders. But his face hurt too much to refuse the suggestion.

Kingston knelt down in the cool, muddy grass and cupped his hands. He submerged them into the cool water and splashed his face. Immediately, he felt relief.

Then, as suddenly as the relief had come, Kingston's heart exploded into a pounding drumbeat of terror. All the muscles in his body tensed. Sweat ran down his chest.

A snake rose from out of the lake, lifted its head higher and higher, and stared with beady black eyes at Kingston. It opened its mouth and hissed. Kingston saw a pink, fleshy, fanged mouth; and the impervious beady eyes staring at him.

"Beware your stupidity, boy. You know nothing about anything. Listen to the words of the forest. It existed before you. It will remain long after you have departed this earth. Ssssstupid boy!"

In a flash, the reptilian body of black and brown diamonds sucked itself back into the lake.

Then all was still.

Kingston picked himself up and walked over to Wiley. "All right, let's try it your way. You better be right about Lucinda. She better know what she's talking about."

CHAPTER 5

Wiley led the way back down the forest path to his home. He had the feeling that things had changed since his first mission with Elden. He was not the only person controlling this new mission. There were six other boys, and they did not all think alike. Destiny was, in some ways, in the hands of their cooperation.

Wiley knew nothing about the snake.

The boys walked through the forest, listening to the scampering of animals in the underbrush, birds singing high up in the canopy, and wind moving gently through the leaves. They did not speak to each other. Neil hugged his doll tightly under his arm and fought back tears.

When they reached the edge of the woods, Wiley carefully peeked out to look at his house.

"Everything looks quiet. But I never know when my father will be home. We're going to have to run quickly and quietly to the tree house. Got it?"

Neil's lower lip trembled. "I can't run that fast."

"Nevin, hold Neil's hand. Don't drag him; but help him run fast."

Nevin grabbed Neil's hand and held it firmly.

"All right … Now! Go!"

The seven boys burst from the woods like a wild beast. Nevin ran with Neil, but they lagged behind. As the larger first group whooshed past Wiley's house, the front door opened.

Wiley heard the creaking door. His heart skipped a series of beats. He felt as though removed from his body. His face blanched whiter than usual, and made the freckles stand out more visibly on his nose and cheeks.

"Where do you think you're going?"

Wiley heard the voice. It wasn't his father's; but he couldn't identify it. Blood pumped through his ears, making him somewhat deaf. Realizing he had no real choice, he stopped and turned slowly around.

It was Mrs. Bannon!

"Hi, Mrs. Bannon."

The other boys stopped in their tracks. They turned around and faced Wiley's neighbor. Mrs. Bannon, the giver of food and shelter. They wanted to see such a miraculous being.

Mrs. Bannon was an old woman with white hair and clouded green eyes. She was short and hunched over from the weight of many hard years. But she held a basket and had a warm twinkle in her eyes.

"Wiley, what are you doing?"

"I'm playing with some friends."

"Playing? Where have you been?"

Wiley looked at his house to see if anyone else would exit the door.

"At the beach. Has my father been home lately?"

"Yes. He was worried about you and asked me to keep an eye out for you."

"My father noticed that I was gone?" Wiley paused. "For how many days now hasn't he seen me?"

"Wiley, don't play games. He's been looking for you for several weeks."

"Well, I've been home. You know my father, Mrs. Bannon. He drinks and forgets things. And he isn't home much himself, you know."

"I know. I know. Poor boy. Well, I put some food in your cupboards. More cheese and some bread."

"Oh, thank you, Mrs. Bannon." Wiley looked furtively at the house. "Do you know where my father is now?"

"Well, he headed toward town. I'm not sure where he was going."

Wiley figured that most likely his father had headed for the tavern. After Mrs. Bannon left, he could go safely into the house and take the bread and cheese.

Mrs. Bannon squinted at the boys. Her eyesight was not good; but something looked wrong. She pointed at the group of boys behind Wiley. "What are they wearing? Are some of them not wearing pants?" Mrs. Bannon blessed herself by making the sign of the cross.

"Oh. They're visiting in town, Mrs. Bannon. They're practicing for a Church play. Where they come from, their Church has costumes."

"Oh." There was silence that seemed to last an eon. "Well, then, go on. Have a nice day."

Mrs. Bannon turned away from the boys and hobbled toward the road. When she had been gone a few minutes, the boys rushed toward the house. Wiley stopped them.

"Go to the tree house! Don't be foolish! You can't risk getting caught. Not everyone here is as blind, or as understanding, as Mrs. Bannon. I'll get the food."

The boys stared at Wiley.

"Go! And don't eat anything in the tree house until I get there!"

Keegan spoke up, "He's right. Let's go."

This time, the boys listened to Keegan. They walked to the tree house and climbed the ladder, one at a time. Nevin went first, then reached out his hand for Neil. Arthur hoisted Neil part way up the ladder.

When they got inside the tree house, Kingston headed for the food. He opened the wooden chest and grabbed a piece of cake. He shoved it into his mouth.

Arthur stomped over to Kingston, forcing his right hand into a fist.

"Listen, Kingston, stop it! We're guests here. If we get thrown out, I don't know where we'll go. Wipe those crumbs off your face and act like you didn't do it!"

Kingston stared defiantly at Arthur while he slowly wiped the crumbs off his face with the back of his hand. "All right. I didn't do it."

The boys sat down at the wooden table and on the top of the wooden chest. Keegan stood up and paced the room. He opened a set of shutters that faced Wiley's house. He was struck by the simple beauty of the place.

Flowers blossomed in a profusion of color throughout the deep emerald green grass - splashes of red, yellow, purple, and pink. Trees grew everywhere, tall trees that stood firmly in the ground and reached into heaven itself. Birds, on wings of bright blue and red and black, flew from tree to tree, singing songs and yelling warnings.

And then there was the house. It fit here, cozily and comfortably. The square structure made from gray and white stone. A rock island in a sea of green.

And, off in the distance, the real sea. The smell of salt and seaweed floating in the air. The sound of waves crashing steadily against the rocks and breaking into froth.

This was not a bad place. This would not be a bad place to live. If one had to.

CHAPTER 6

Keegan closed the shutters and moved back inside. Moments later, he heard footsteps ascending the tree house ladder. The door flew open, slammed shut, and Wiley stepped inside.

“Here. I got it!”

Wiley held two loaves of bread and a block of cheese in his left arm. He walked over to the wooden chest and asked the boys seated there to get up.

“I’m going to put this newer food in here. We’ll eat the older food first.”

Wiley noticed crumbs and a small chunk of cake lying in the bottom of the chest. He was fairly certain that those had not been there when they had put the food away and closed the lid. He debated what to do. He decided not to address the issue directly. Kingston and Arthur seemed angry and on edge. Neil was close to tears much of the time. He would hint at the problem and see that rules were laid down.

“We need to have a meeting, boys.”

Neil looked at Wiley with large, widened eyes. Arthur and Kingston rolled their eyes toward the tree house ceiling.

Keegan spoke first. “A meeting? About what?’

"To make some rules. Lucinda told us that we are to meet with Elden. But he may not come right away. Until then, we have limited food and we need to preserve it."

Kingston glared at Wiley. "Limited food? I see vegetables in your backyard! And you know, there must be animals around here to hunt."

"What? Vegetables?" Wiley had completely forgotten that he and his father had planted vegetables. "Where?"

Kingston walked to a set of window shutters facing Wiley's house and opened them. He pointed to a small patch of green leaves. "There!"

"My word …" Wiley stared at the patch. Carrot leaves! He recognized them from Mrs. Bannon's garden. Under the ground, there would be carrots!

Kingston continued, "You hunt down an animal, prepare it, add it to the carrots, and you have food!"

Wiley thought about what was involved. "Please shut the window, Kingston."

Kingston closed the window, leaned against the wall and crossed his arms. He waited for Wiley's next words.

"That is all fine and good. We have carrots. You think that we can hunt animals. But we need variety in our food. We need to preserve cheese and bread and all of the other food until Elden meets with us."

"Until Elden meets with us? You're leaving your fate up to a dolphin?"

Calder stood up, walked around the room, and positioned himself between Kingston and Wiley. “Look. Let’s calm down and think about this. We were rescued from our city under the ocean by Wiley and the dolphin. Maybe Wiley knows what he’s talking about.”

Keegan spoke up, “I’ve been thinking the same thing. We were hit by a meteor. Then Wiley shows up and rescues us on the back of a dolphin. Then we do nothing but argue with him. Maybe we should listen to him!”

Neil looked from Calder to Keegan, then at Wiley. “I want to see my mother. Can you help me?”

Wiley looked down at the floor. He noticed suddenly a variety of patterns in the polished wood. “I don’t know. We’ll have to see what Elden has in mind.”

Arthur looked at Wiley. “I apologize for our behavior.” He looked at Kingston. “I think that we are very upset over what has happened to us. We don’t know where our families are. We don’t know what has happened to them. You lead the way. Tell us what you want us to do next.”

Keegan shook his head in agreement. “Yes! Tell us what we need to do next to return to our families.”

Wiley lifted his gaze from the floor. He looked around the room at each and every boy. He brought his gaze to rest on Keegan. “We need the golden cup given to you by Lucinda. Where is it?”

“In the blanket I’ve been using for sleeping.”

"Good. We need to take that down to the beach. We need to walk into the shallow water and hold it underwater. When Elden sees it, he'll come to meet with us."

Keegan answered, "Then that's what we'll do. I want to start tomorrow morning."

A small smile appeared momentarily on Wiley's face. He looked again at the wooden floor. "Good. Tomorrow is perfect."

There was silence then among the boys. They all sat together in thought. Keegan opened the windows facing away from Wiley's house. For hours, the boys listened to the pounding of the ocean surf against the shoreline. Birds sang overhead. At some point, a bird with a yellow beak and bright blue wings landed on a branch outside the windows. He peered inside the house with deep black eyes. He moved his head up-and-down and sideways, trying to take in all that he could about the boys in the tree house.

Neil found his blanket, unfolded it and placed it on top of the food chest. He lay down, crossed his arms behind his head and watched out the window. He looked at the deep green tree leaves dancing in the wind, their soft brown spines bending in the breeze. He listened to the bird singing. He thought, how odd that he and the other boys were in a cage while the bird was free.

He hoped that Wiley and Elden could lead them all back home. He missed his parents. He missed the city. He missed his everyday life back home.

CHAPTER 7

The next day, the boys once again woke up in the tree house. The sun filtered in through the shutters, as it had done the previous morning. Sunshine splashed across the wooden table and onto the floor. Wiley stirred as the sun trickled behind his eyelids.

When all the boys had woken up, Wiley announced, "Today is the day. Let's eat breakfast, pack a lunch for all of us, and head on down to the beach."

The boys bustled about, folding up their blankets and putting them away.

Keegan thought suddenly of something, "What should we wear?"

Wiley looked at him blankly.

"I mean, do we wear our tunics?"

"Oh, that. Well, how about anyone who can fit into my clothes, probably Keegan, Calder, and Nevin … and Neil can wear my older clothes … they should wear my clothes. Then only Arthur and Kingston are left." Wiley looked first at Arthur, then at Kingston. "You can wear your tunics. But bring blankets that you can wrap around yourselves. If we're caught, we can use the shipwreck story. If you're caught wearing your tunics, we'll try the church play story again."

Arthur nodded in agreement. Kingston turned away and walked toward the food chest. He lifted the lid. "Let's start packing food for our day at the beach."

Wiley responded, "Why don't you take care of that, Kingston? I'll pick out some food for breakfast."

Wiley thought that everyone should be fortified and strong for what might turn out to be a long day. He remembered how long he had waited for Elden the first time. He grabbed a large loaf of bread, a wheel of cheese, strawberries, blackberry jam, a container of juice, and an entire rich, sweet cake. He placed them all on the table.

Neil jumped up and down and clapped his hands. His golden curls bobbed every which way on his head. His hazel eyes glistened with excitement. He was the first to grab a chair. He scrambled up on top of it, folded his spindly legs underneath himself, and reached across the table. Before anyone could say anything, he ripped off a huge chunk of cake, lifted it to his mouth and took a bite. He murmured to himself as he chewed and savored the sweet substance.

The older boys stared at Neil, about to express six different complaints. But, before their thoughts could turn into words, they realized how utterly content and happy Neil was at that moment. They decided to allow him the piece of cake. Besides, he had already taken a huge bite out of it.

CHAPTER 8

After breakfast, the boys climbed down the ladder from the tree house. Wiley went first. He felt the rough, weatherworn steps on his hands and feet. They were nothing more than boards nailed into the tree. When Wiley's bare feet hit the ground, he looked up to see a bundled blanket tied to a stick descending toward him. It was the day's food, all neatly wrapped up in a gray blanket and ready for carrying.

After the food, came Neil. He was chewing on a piece of candy. In one hand, he carried the doll that Wiley had given him. He used the other hand and his feet to navigate down the ladder. Wiley put the food package on the ground and stood beneath the steps to help Neil.

Neil looked so different, as though he were a new boy in a new century, vaguely related to the person he used to be. He wore Wiley's old clothes from when he was slightly older than Neil. He wore a plain white, short sleeve shirt and brown pants with a hole in the knee. His face was dirty and his golden, curly hair disheveled. He looked like any other child in Wiley's village. When he had first arrived on the island, he had looked so different, wearing his tunic, a toga trimmed in red stripes, and his red shoes. Now he looked ragged but feisty, ready to take on the world.

Wiley watched the other boys descend from the tree house. It was like watching people from two different eras. Arthur and Kingston wore their tunics. They looked misplaced in time, or as though dressed in costume for a performance. But all of the other boys looked like they belonged in the village.

Nevin wore old, dark blue pants and a faded gray shirt. The pants were too short for him, rising above his ankles. The shirt was also small, revealing Nevin's stomach. Calder wore a tan shirt that was too tight for him and faded brown pants. His red hair was tousled and falling onto his forehead.

Keegan was the biggest surprise. He no longer looked like royalty. He wore a light blue, short sleeve shirt with a torn collar. His borrowed gray pants were too short for him and had holes in both knees. He had bare feet. His long, golden hair was knotted and messy. He looked like any other child in Wiley's village. If all of the neighbors didn't know each other, Keegan could have easily become lost in a crowd.

Wiley wondered if it was that easy to move to another place, or another period in time. Just change your clothing and blend in.

CHAPTER 9

The boys walked down to the beach. Neil ran ahead, delighted with the world around him. He ran barefoot along the sandy path that led from Wiley's backyard to the beach. He slapped the soles of his feet on long, flattened, green stalks of grass. He kicked sand into the air and let it slide between his toes. He chased after butterflies. He spent time picking small, red wildflowers that grew along the way. He pushed a bunch of the brightly colored flowers against his nose and breathed in the perfume. He smiled and laughed at the fragrance.

Wiley thought how easily this child had become lost in time. No worries. No cares. It was as though Neil felt he would be reunited with his parents and his home simply by going to the beach.

Wiley realized that his own fate had been sealed in this regard. He would never see his mother again, no matter how far he traveled.

When the boys reached the beach, Wiley walked over to the large black rock he had visited on so many earlier days. He placed the gray knapsack there, then climbed back down. He spoke to the waiting boys.

"This is where I first met Elden." Wiley gestured toward the ocean. "He wouldn't meet with me until I had the golden cup and dipped it underwater. We're going to need a golden goblet this time as well, I'm sure."

Keegan spoke next, "Did you place it in the knapsack?"

"Yes. Whenever you're ready, you can have it. You want to try it right away?"

"Sure."

Keegan scaled the black rock and unfolded the knapsack. There it was. One of the goblets he remembered so well from home. Golden and generously decorated with sparkling gems. Engraved with a dolphin on either end of the line of words: "Drink deeply by land or sea. Earth comes only once."

Keegan had always wondered what those words meant. All of the times that he and his family and dinner guests had drunk liquid from the golden vessels. Suddenly, the words made sense. At least for now. He felt the need to live life deeply - by land, or by sea, or wherever. Life was short. He hoped that his family was still alive. He hoped once again to see the city where he lived.

Keegan grabbed the cup and ran barefoot down the large, rough rock. He ran out onto the sand to join the other boys. He handed the cup to Wiley.

"Here. Show us what to do."

"No. You take it. Lucinda said that you should dip it into the ocean. Just wave it around under the water where Elden can see it."

Keegan clutched the golden stem of the goblet. He felt power melt from the cup into his hand. He felt reunited with his family, his city, his time period. He looked away from Wiley and out to sea.

As he walked to the water's edge, he had the feeling of déjà vu. All looked so familiar. The blue-green water, the pure white froth that rolled itself into curls and tumbled toward the beach. The gigantic black rocks that stood like small islands in the liquid emerald sea. The brilliance of the sun as it broke upon the water and shimmered in all directions.

Keegan looked at the far horizon. Clouds in many shapes floated across the clear blue sky. He remembered spending long hours as a young child looking up into the clouds, finding shapes of things he knew. As he thought about this, he absentmindedly noticed a whale floating by, then a horse, then a chariot.

Keegan turned and looked at the profile of the beach. The shoreline had changed. It was a different shape. It had once been a nearly straight line. Now the edge of the sand looked more like a long ribbon waving in the breeze, jutting in and out of the water.

Was this really his former island? Or was this some type of incredible trick?

Choosing not to question something he couldn't answer at this point in time, Keegan turned back toward the ocean and waded into the shallow water. He let the froth run over his feet until he was used to the cool temperature. Then he walked out until the ocean was as deep as his waist.

Keegan waved the golden goblet back and forth under the water. Nothing. No dolphin. Nothing. Once a large clump of seaweed covered Keegan's feet. That was it.

After an hour, Keegan walked back on land. His legs felt heavy as he moved through the water. As his feet touched dry sand, he waved to Wiley who had been watching him retreat from the ocean.

Keegan yelled to Wiley, "Nothing! No dolphin came! Nothing!"

Wiley looked out to sea. Calm and still. Quiet broken only by the gentle roll of surf and the occasional seagull flying overhead.

"Well, it happens that way sometimes. Elden only comes when he's ready. I think he tests people. Makes sure they're patient and strong enough for his missions."

Keegan dropped his arm and dangled the golden cup by its stem. He banged it gently against his leg.

"Why don't you try it?"

"No. I think that Elden meant for you to do this. You have to be patient."

The boys spent the rest of the day at the beach. Wiley built another sand replica of the castle he had seen on his journey with Father Muldowney. Neil used small, broken pieces of twigs as army men and invaded the castle.

Nevin dug a deep hole in front of the castle. He then filled it with water by repeatedly taking a hollow log down to the ocean's edge. He filled the log with incoming froth and water, then ran it back to the hole. When he had dumped enough liquid into the pit to fill it, Nevin said, “There, Neil, now you have an ocean in front of your castle.”

Arthur had watched in amusement as the castle was built, then the ocean constructed. “You need boats, Neil.” Arthur scoured the beach for seashells. When he had found ten lightweight seashells, perfectly curved along the bottom, he returned to the miniature castle. He placed the delicate seashells, all white and smooth and laced with the barest hint of colors, blue and pink and orange, in the sand next to Neil.

Neil looked up into Arthur’s face with twinkling eyes and a large smile. “Thank you, Arthur.”

Then Neil set to work, sending his boats out into the miniature sea, and giving orders to his tiny stick men. He played for hours that way.

The older boys took turns going out into the real ocean, waving the cup underwater. Wiley insisted that only Keegan should use the goblet that way; but the boys wouldn’t listen. Finally, Keegan took a second turn.

After thirty minutes, he gave up and returned to shore. No dolphin.

The boys ate whenever they were hungry. They scrambled up onto the large rock that held the knapsack of food and chose whatever they wanted to eat. Mid-afternoon, Nevin came back with food for Neil - a chunk of cheese and a large torn piece of bread covered in strawberry jam. He also brought him a small flask of water, and told his brother to drink.

Neil guzzled the water and wolfed down the food. He thanked Nevin and then ran down to the ocean's edge to cool off. He sat on the wet sand, and giggled as the cool water covered his legs, then retreated back to its depths.

The boys spent the entire day at the beach. At sunset, they sat on the beach and observed the end of day.

The sun dropped from the sky slowly, becoming more and more golden in its descent. Ribbons of fire unfurled across the sky - orange, pink, and yellow. Clouds burst into flame. Burning ashes spilled across the ocean, glittering in the deepening blue. The black rocks stood silently, morphing into silhouettes as day turned into night.

Keegan climbed up onto the large black rock that held the knapsack before the water reached it. He unfolded the blanket and discovered that all but one chunk of bread had been eaten. He grabbed the sack and returned to the boys.

"Well, what do you want to do? Go back to the tree house?"

There was silence. Then Arthur spoke, "I think I'd rather stay here. Sleep here. What do you all think?"

Neil started jumping up and down and running in circles through the wet sand. "Sleep on the beach! Sleep on the beach! Let's do it! Please! Please! Please! Let's sleep on the beach!"

When the older boys did not answer him immediately, Neil ran down to the water's edge, slapping his feet through the shallow water slipping onto land. He stopped when he came upon a jellyfish that had washed ashore. He studied the clear body and the remnants of luminescence still sparking through the jelly. He turned to call out to Nevin; but noticed that the older boys were huddled together in discussion.

Neil turned back to the jellyfish and studied it more closely. When the ocean water moved against it, green sparks lit up a section of the jelly. Delighted with his discovery, Neil searched around for a rock or a shell. When he found a stick, he grabbed that instead.

He poked the jellyfish. Each time he did so, green light flashed in the spot that had been disturbed. It was like nudging a dying creature back to life. Neil continued to do this until he could no longer produce light with his effort. Then he turned back toward the older boys and trudged through wet, and then dry, sand to reach them.

As he approached the group, Nevin turned to Neil. "Neil, guess what? We're going to sleep on the beach tonight!"

"Really?" Neil jumped up and down and asked where he would sleep.

"Wiley, Arthur and Kingston are going back to the tree house for blankets, more food, and anything else we might need. We'll decide exactly where we'll camp when they get back."

Calder interrupted. "We're building a fire on the beach tonight, Neil. You'll like that!"

Neil smiled. "Thanks, Nevin." He put his hand in Nevin's and stood still for a few minutes, thinking about the night ahead of them. He watched as the last remnant of sun dropped from the face of earth and disappeared into the deep abyss behind the sea. Then he let go of Nevin's hand and went to play with his sandcastle and boats and military men. His men would need to take cover in the castle this night.

CHAPTER 10

As a white, luminous full moon traveled upward in the deep black sky, stars scattered like diamonds across the canopy. Wiley, Arthur and Kingston found their way back down to the beach, laden with blankets, food and dry clothes, by the light of the moon.

When they reached the sand, Wiley instructed Arthur and Kingston to place everything as far back from the incoming tide as possible. They walked a short distance onto the beach and put everything down in a neat pile.

Kingston put his fingers into his mouth and blew out a shrill whistle in order to call the other boys.

Wiley grabbed his arm. "You can't do that! We don't want anyone to hear us! We don't want to be found out down here!"

"Oh, right. I'm sorry."

Keegan, Nevin, Neil and Calder heeded the whistle and sauntered across the sand. When all the boys were together, Wiley spoke first.

"We're going to camp here tonight, right on this spot. It's far enough away from the incoming tide."

Keegan spoke next, "Won't people in your village be able to see a fire here?"

"No. I've built fires down here before. You can't even see them from my house. The trees block the view. We just have to be careful not to make too much smoke."

Arthur asked, "Where do we find firewood? Where's the best place to look?"

"Over there." Wiley pointed toward the part of the forest closest to the beach. "Don't go deep into the forest. Just go in a little way, and collect broken branches. There are wolves and at least one bear in the forest, so just stay toward the edge."

Neil's eyes grew large.

Wiley realized what he had said. "Don't worry, Neil. The bears and wolves never come out to the beach. I've never seen them outside the forest. They like it in there."

Neil absorbed the information quietly. He sat down on the sand and wrapped his arms together under his knees. He watched the froth of the ocean waves glowing in the moonlight, curling upward toward the heavens and then crashing back down to earth. In the deep blackness far out to sea, it looked like ghosts moving in the night. Neil shivered and asked his older brother for a blanket. Nevin grabbed a gray woolen one and wrapped it around Neil. After watching the ocean for awhile, Neil hugged himself with the blanket and lay down in the sand to watch the stars.

Wiley turned to Nevin, and then to the other boys. "Nevin, I think that you should stay here with Neil. I think that everyone else should come with me, so that we can collect enough firewood in one quick trip."

All of the boys shook their heads in agreement, except for Neil who just looked briefly at Wiley and then back toward the stars exploding into view along the horizon.

"All right. Let's go."

The boys assigned to collect firewood followed Wiley. They walked through the dry sand. It was still warm, but beginning to cool. The boys sank into the sand a bit and felt the dry crystal grains wash between their toes. They moved on, listening to the waves rumble and growl and crash into the hard, wet sand down at the shoreline.

Calder watched his shadow move beneath the full moon. He smelled the salty air and felt it bathe his skin. He watched as the stars ignited pinpoint holes in the blackened sky. Although he missed home deeply, he could not remember a time of greater freedom. A time when he did not need to report to adults. When he did not need to go to bed early in preparation for school lessons the next day.

Kingston was the first to speak, "It's beautiful out here."

Wiley thought about that. "Yes, it really is."

"Do you often come out here at night?"

"Sometimes; but not often. Since my mother died, I come out more often than I used to. It's comforting."

Calder answered him, "Yes, it is. It's so different from home; and yet it's very much the same."

"What do you mean?" Wiley looked puzzled.

"The ocean looks the same as it does near our city. Something about the color of the water and the look of the beach. I don't know what it is. The shoreline is so different; but something about it is the same. Ours is basically a straight line. Yours wanders in and out."

Keegan interrupted him. "You noticed that, too? I had been thinking earlier that our shoreline is a straight line, and that this one looks like a long ribbon waving in the breeze. But there's something about the beach and the ocean here that looks so much like home."

Wiley let the pounding crash of the surf absorb his thoughts for a few minutes before he spoke. "Do you know exactly where you are?"

Keegan answered him, "What do you mean?"

"Do you understand where you are, exactly?"

"In some small village by the sea."

"Is that all? Do you know what time period this is? Do you know how you got here?"

The boys walked through the darkness illuminated by the light of the moon. The surf pounded against the land. Shadows danced at the edge of the forest, imitating the trees dancing in the evening breeze. The boys' shadows followed closely along beside them, as though an extra team of helpers had come to help them.

After a few moments' silence, Keegan answered Wiley, "We arrived here on the backs of a dolphin and a whale. Supposedly we came from a city that existed centuries before yours. Supposedly everyone else in our civilization has died."

Wiley looked at Keegan with his mouth open wide for a few seconds. When he spoke, only one word escaped his lips, "Supposedly?"

"Well, I mean, how likely is it that we've survived for centuries?"

Wiley thought about this. Keegan had a good point. "It's not very likely. That's why this is so amazing and must be treated with great reverence. I take this very seriously."

Kingston interrupted. "Think about this. We did ride on the backs of a dolphin and a whale. We did travel to a very different place this way. But we've talked about this, and we don't believe that we've come centuries forward in time."

Kingston looked Wiley straight in the eye, and then down at the ground. He was momentarily distracted by a patch of seaweed sprawled out against the sand in the shape of a snake. Kingston shook his head. It was his imagination playing tricks on him.

Wiley realized that the boys had been talking to each other when he wasn't present. At least some of them had arrived at the conclusion that he wasn't telling the truth. Wiley remained silent and thought about his options.

The boys walked along the beach, sifting sand between their toes. They listened to the waves rising up, and then smashing apart once they reached land. They noticed dying jellyfish sparkling in the moonlight and seaweed littered among old, used shells. They moved onward toward the forest.

As he walked, Wiley realized that the only way to prove to the boys that he was telling the truth was through Elden. Until Elden showed up, there was nothing he could do. The boys would either believe him or not; but still he was responsible for them.

When they reached the forest, Wiley told the boys where to find wood, "Don't go deep into the forest. It isn't necessary. This far away from the ocean, we'll find all the dry wood we need close to the edge. Deeper into the forest, there are a lot of wild animals."

Kingston turned to Wiley with half a smile playing across his lips. "Like what?"

"Like wolves, a bear, things you don't want to see."

Kingston continued to smile as he looked at the forest. The edge was sparse. He could see between the trees. But, farther in, it looked impenetrable. He could see nothing but a moving wall of leaves dancing in the wind.

"Well, let's go."

Kingston marched ahead and led the way into the forest. As the boys gathered branches and logs in their arms, they heard the howl of a wolf. Calder accidentally dropped most of his wood.

"What was that?"

Wiley answered him, "A wolf. You'll hear them at night. As far as I know, they've never come out this far. When I traveled through the forest at night, I heard them many times. But I never actually saw them, not even in the forest."

Kingston looked sideways at Wiley. "So why can't we go deeper into the woods?"

"I ran into a bear in there at night. Later, I came across it near some caves. I had to kill it with a spear I made. The bear's cub is still alive within the woods; and it's grown now."

Kingston laughed. "You made a spear and killed a bear with it?"

Wiley glared at Kingston. "Yes. Now can we just get the wood and go back to our spot on the beach and build a fire?"

The boys worked in silence, gathering wood. They worked for almost an hour, each to their own thoughts.

CHAPTER 11

After the logs and branches were piled up and set aflame, Wiley produced food from within a knapsack. He divided a block of cheese among the boys and passed around a container of apple juice. Then he taught them how to lightly toast bread on sticks over an open flame. As they warmed the bread, Wiley produced a large jar of blackberry jam for smothering the bread with extra flavor.

After they ate, the boys sat for a long time around the campfire, watching the wood turn red hot, then crackle and spit and fall to ashes. Keegan imagined in the dancing, ever changing shadows, the shapes of people he knew: his mother, father, cousins, neighbors. His gaze returned to the fire. As he watched, a fiery red ember fell from a log and floated down to the ash.

Keegan remembered the meteor. The screaming. The running. He stood up and kicked sand toward the ocean.

"I'm going to sleep now. Where's a blanket I can use?"

Wiley handed a white woolen blanket to Keegan. He spread it open on the ground a short distance from the fire and folded it so that he could slip inside and cover himself. Within moments of lying down, he fell fast asleep.

A short while later, the other boys followed suit and crawled into soft, folded beds under the stars. Nevin spread out a blanket for Neil who had fallen asleep in the sand playing a game with sticks and seashells. He carried Neil over to the blanket, covered him up, and then arranged his own bed next to him. Within moments, all of the boys were sound asleep.

The surf pounded rhythmically. The fire sputtered and crackled. From a distance, wolves howled within the forest. Around the campfire, seven boys slept and dreamed and breathed quietly into the night air.

Neil stood up and looked around. He wondered when everyone had gone to sleep. He looked at the vast darkness in front of him. As his eyes focused, he saw the long, broken lines of whitecaps floating up and down. Lit by the full moon, they glowed like ghosts moving in the night. He decided to go down to the water and investigate.

As Neil placed his toes, then his feet, then all of himself up to his waist in the cold, salty water, he started to cry. He wanted to see his parents, his city, all of his neighborhood friends. How had he come here to this unfamiliar island? How could he go back?

As he cried and turned himself in circles, Neil felt something strong and slippery brush against his legs. Filled with panic, he froze. He discovered that he could not scream. Rooted to one spot, moved only by the strong ocean current, Neil saw a dolphin rise up in front of him. The dolphin stood on its tail and danced backward. Then Neil heard the dolphin tell him to climb up on his back and hang onto his fin.

Neil scrambled up onto the dolphin's back and grabbed onto his top fin. Then the dolphin pulled him under the inky, murky waves. He swam deeper.

Neil's eyes adjusted to the dark in a way that they had never done before. He saw the ocean floor drop away as they moved farther out to sea. He noticed fish of various colors: yellow, red, silver, blue. He heard humpback whales singing in the distance.

"Where are we going?"

"Home, Neil. You can visit. Tomorrow we'll all go back to your city."

Neil hugged the dolphin and held him tightly.

As they reached a place deep in the ocean, Neil saw a huge glowing light. In a flash, for a second or two, he saw a large beast with the head of a snake standing in front of a golden gate and a broken stone wall. It reminded Neil of his city. He squeezed the dolphin and stared at the scene before him.

Then the beast, the gate, and the wall shimmered in front of him and disappeared. A puff of purple smoke arose from the ocean floor, swirled like a tornado, and likewise disappeared into the deep, glassy water. Neil's city came into view. The water vanished.

Neil grasped the golden bars of the city's front gate. He wondered how he had gotten outside. He tried to open the gate; but discovered that it was locked. As he leaned against it, the gate suddenly gave way and opened.

Neil pushed the golden bars forward and stepped into his city. As he entered, the gate slammed safely closed behind him.

CHAPTER 12

"Neil, come on! Sit down! Can't we finish the game?"

Neil wondered why he was standing in front of the fountain near the city's front gate. He must have wandered over, mesmerized by the water, he told himself. This fountain was one of his favorite places in the entire city. He looked up at the statue of the woman gazing toward the heavens while pouring water from two vases, one in each hand. He looked at the tiles painted with pictures of flowers that surrounded the fountain.

"Come on, Neil!"

Neil looked over at the three boys playing on the courtyard cobblestone. His three best friends: Garrett Lyons, Jackson O'Birn, and Rafferty MacCuinn. Garrett was throwing toy knucklebones and dice into the air, listening to their small echo throughout the courtyard as he waited for his friend to rejoin them.

Garrett was short and pudgy. He had golden, straight hair that fell to his ears. He had green eyes, freckles, and chubby hands. Jackson was the opposite: thin and tall and athletic. He had black hair, blue eyes, and ruddy cheeks. Rafferty had golden, curly hair like Neil's, dark brown eyes and thick black eyelashes. He was of medium height and build, but unusually strong for his size.

Neil walked over to his friends. What had they been playing? He couldn't believe that he had become so distracted, he had forgotten. Had they been playing knucklebones? It didn't look like it. Garrett was throwing knucklebones and his favorite dice made from blue stone into the air; but there were other toys on the ground - terracotta toy soldiers and chariots, along with a multitude of colored dice and knucklebones.

Rafferty looked up from his attempt to build a wall with dice. "Come on. You can be on my side. Help me build a wall to protect our soldiers."

Neil ran over to join Rafferty. Soldiers was one of his favorite games!

"Sure. I'll play!"

Jackson looked up, quickly shading his eyes with his hand to block out the onslaught of sun. "Oh, sure, now you'll play. When you can be on Rafferty's side!"

"He's building a wall! Your men are totally exposed to the enemy!"

Jackson smiled. "Well, that's true! Here, Rafferty, give me some dice!"

The dice and knucklebones belonged to Rafferty. He collected them because he liked the shapes and colors. They reminded him of polished stones which he also collected; but the square dice could be stacked in order to build things.

Rafferty handed twelve dice to Jackson. "Here. See what you can build with these."

Jackson built a small wall with the tiny bricks of dice in various colors: turquoise, red, yellow, gray. Then he positioned his terracotta soldiers behind the wall. He grabbed two chariots and lined them up behind the soldiers next to a pile of swords. When the time came, his men would jump into the chariots and ride courageously into battle.

With Garrett sitting next to Jackson, and Neil and Rafferty sitting directly across from them, the boys played soldiers in the cobblestone courtyard. They played for over an hour, trying to determine the fate of the miniature terracotta soldiers.

As mealtime approached, Neil's mother walked into the courtyard.

"Hey, Neil. It's time to eat."

Suddenly, Neil realized that he was extraordinarily happy to see his mother and very hungry. He dropped the toys in his hand onto the courtyard stone and ran to hug her. He threw his arms around her.

Neil's mother was a tall, thin, pleasant woman. Her golden hair was wrapped in a bun at the top of her head. She wore a light blue tunic that fell to her ankles and a gray shawl over her shoulders. The shawl fell into her bent arms as she hugged her son.

"I have a wonderful lunch prepared for you!"

"What is it?"

"Let's make it a surprise. Come on."

Neil broke away from his mother's embrace. He turned to his friends. "Bye. See you later." Then he ran from the courtyard, shouting over his shoulder to his mother, "I'll race you home."

His mother laughed. "You already won! See you at home!"

Neil ran through the city streets - two blocks straight, three blocks to the right - to his house. He was incredibly happy to see his home. His family lived upstairs. His father owned a bookstore on the first floor. His family also rented out two rooms with a separate entrance on the first floor.

When Neil reached the bookstore, he pulled open the front door and took in the surroundings slowly, as though trying to appreciate them fully. The walls were made from white concrete decorated with swirling circular patterns. On the outside of the building, stones had been set into the concrete. Two years ago, Neil's father had painted the front door red.

Inside, most of the store contained wooden bookshelves displaying both new and older books. On the right-hand side, a small section had been devoted to tables and chairs where customers could read. Neil noticed that two actors from the city were seated at different tables, studying two of the older books.

Neil liked the musty smell of the old books. It suggested to him that these books had a history. They had been written by people who had lived in another time. When the books were new, the world was different.

In the back of the store was a counter where customers could purchase their selections. Neil saw from the front door that his father was seated behind the counter, reading a book. He ran through the aisle that divided the bookshelves from the reading section and yelled to his father.

"Hi, Father!"

The actors looked up.

"Hi, Neil. Quiet. We have customers."

Neil's father was a tall, thin, quiet man. He had black hair, a moustache, and thick black hair on his arms and legs. His brown eyes twinkled as he smiled at Neil.

"Your mother cooked you a wonderful lunch. Why don't you go up and see?"

As Neil headed for the stairs along the side wall, directly behind the reading tables, his father called out to him, "Your cousins, Julian and Helen, are visiting."

"Really? How wonderful! No one told me!"

Neil raced up the stairs. His Aunt Chloe met him at the upstairs door.

"Hi, Neil. I heard you coming up the stairs. You sound like two galloping horses. How are customers supposed to read?" Neil's aunt laughed. "There are two actors studying their lines downstairs. Did you see them?"

"Yes. Yes, I did."

Chloe, the sister of Neil's mother, was small, dainty, seven years younger than Neil's mother, and a pleasure to have around. Easygoing and happy by nature, she was fascinated by the arts. When Neil was four years old, she had taken him into the heart of the city to watch a children's play put on by street performers. He still remembered the costumes, and the makeup, and the way in which they had made their voices extra loud. He hoped to see another play this year. His aunt and mother had been discussing it.

Neil looked away from his Aunt Chloe toward his cousins who were sitting at the kitchen table. He took in the entire room, again as though trying to fully appreciate all that was around him.

The upstairs apartment was sparsely decorated. The front door opened into the kitchen. It had the same cement walls with circular designs as the bookstore did. Directly across from the door was a large masonry stove. Bronze pots and pans hung on the wall next to the stove. Fire danced in two of the six burners, heating one large pot and one small pot. Firelight bounced from the bronze pots, filling the cooking area with a warm, inviting glow.

Neil smelled meat and sauce; but he couldn't identify the exact combination. His stomach ached suddenly with unfathomable hunger.

In the center of the room was a large, circular, wooden table surrounded by eight wooden chairs. His cousin Julian sat in one chair, playing with small terracotta soldiers like the ones his friends had had in the courtyard. His cousin Helen sat in another chair, playing with a cloth doll.

Julian was Neil's exact age, six years old. Neil had been born two weeks earlier than Julian. From the day Julian was born, the boys had been together at least three times a week and were more like brothers than cousins.

Although Julian was slightly younger than Neil, he was bigger, stronger, and more active. He often took the lead in games and contests. Julian had soft brown hair. Like Neil, he had hazel eyes.

Helen was three years old. Like her mother, she was small and dainty with golden, curly hair and lucid green eyes. However, rather than the easygoing nature of her mother's personality, Helen had a strong will and a temper that easily ignited.

Not interested in Helen's doll playing, Neil yelled hello to Julian. He ran across the room and sat next to him.

"Can I have some soldiers?"

"Sure."

Julian slid five of his twelve soldiers over to Neil.

"Oh. I want to show you something." Neil ran into his small bedroom off the kitchen. He returned shortly with a handful of stone dice. "Look what Rafferty taught me to do. You can build walls with dice to protect your soldiers!"

Neil dumped the dice onto the table. With a clattering sound, they tumbled toward Julian. He grabbed about twelve dice and passed the remainder to Neil.

"Let's build!"

The two boys built walls and played toy soldiers. Bored and feeling left out, Helen climbed down off her chair. She went over to her mother who was stirring a richly scented meal in a large pot and hugged her long, soft yellow tunic. She rubbed the cloth against her cheek and sucked her thumb. When her mother finished stirring, she placed the copper ladle down on a plate, covered the pot, and picked up her daughter.

Helen rested her head on her mother's shoulder, sucked her thumb and watched the boys play their game. She whimpered briefly and complained that she was hungry.

As Neil played soldiers with his cousin, his mother walked into the apartment. Neil looked up and yelled across the room, "Hi, Mother!"

She answered, "Hello," walked across the room, and rubbed the top of her son's head with affection.

"I've got a delicious lunch prepared."

"What is it?"

"I'm not telling. It will be a surprise."

"I'm starving."

"I'll serve it up right now. Why don't you and Julian clear your toys from the table?"

Because the boys were so hungry, they quickly moved their toys from the table into Neil's bedroom.

Neil's mother removed the lid from the smaller pot, stirred the sauce, and took a deep breath of the pleasant ingredients. She then did the same with the food in the larger pot. Her sister took dishes down from a cabinet shelf and announced that she would set the table.

Neil watched as his aunt placed six shiny bronze plates around the table.

"Six plates? Is father coming upstairs for lunch?"

"Yes. He's closing the shop for lunch today."

"Hurray!"

Neil's mother asked that Chloe carry the plates to her one at a time, so that she could serve the food from the stove.

Neil watched as his mother removed the pots from the burners, placed them on a counter next to the stove, and took off the lids.

"We're having a stew made from pork with lentil beans and garlic sauce. Remember this, Neil? We had it a few months ago."

Neil looked puzzled. "No. But it smells good!"

Chloe served Neil first, then Julian. She gave Helen cheese and bread while she waited, then cut up her meat in a small serving. At three years of age, Helen was a picky eater. She dabbled at meals, and preferred snacks.

As Neil's mother served up the adult portions onto plates, his father walked into the apartment.

"Hi, Father!"

"Hi, Neil! My goodness, smell that food! What a great day to have closed the shop!"

Neil's father sat at the table. Neil's mother placed a meal in front of him. Then she took down six stone goblets from a shelf, filled them with berry juice, and handed them around. Chloe placed a bowl of bread and a plate of sliced cheese on the table, then sat down to eat.

Neil stared mesmerized at the stone goblets. They reminded him of something; but he couldn't place the memory. He had always liked these cups: gray stone swirled with blue and green designs.

"So what did you do today, Neil?"

Neil looked at his father. "Played soldiers with Julian. Before that, I played soldiers with my friends in the front courtyard by the fountain. I learned a trick from Rafferty. You can take dice and stack them to build walls. Then you can hide your soldiers behind them!"

"Very smart. Good strategy."

Neil's father then turned to his mother. "Some of the actors are planning to meet at our bookshop this evening."

"Oh, how wonderful!"

"It should be interesting, and good for business."

Neil's mother turned to her sister who loved the theatre. "Do you want to stop by this evening?"

"I wish I could. I have so much to do at home tonight. Maybe another time."

Neil looked around the table at his family. He realized how extraordinarily happy and content he felt.

CHAPTER 13

Suddenly, in a flash, as though they had never been there, Neil's family and house disappeared. He was alone. Water rushed toward him like a tidal wave and swallowed everything.

Neil was at the bottom of the ocean in darkness. He was standing, peering into liquid nothingness. From a light that pulsed somewhere in the distance, he eventually made out the ruins of a city.

As fear mounted in his chest, a dolphin moved through the water in front of him.

"Get up on my back."

Neil followed his directions, as though he knew exactly what to do. He held onto the dolphin's top fin. As he did that, his vision intensified under water. He lost the incredible chill that had overtaken his small body. He felt warm and suddenly aware of life around him.

He noticed to his right a large, glowing jellyfish. Almost as tall as Neil himself, the top of the jelly appeared to be made from blue webbing; the center was blood red; long white tentacles hung, glowing, from the bottom.

"Don't be afraid, Neil. We're just passing through. You're safe with me."

Neil relaxed. He absorbed everything he could about the world around him.

He gasped unexpectedly as a creature he had thought was a rock buried beneath the sand wriggled out from beneath the grainy cover, rising up like a large snake. It appeared to be sculpted from golden sand and brown rock.

"That's a sea cucumber, Neil. Look over there." Elden moved his head in a direction away from the cucumber.

Neil saw a red spider crawling slowly across the ocean floor.

"What's that?"

"A spider with no eyes."

"No eyes?"

"Think about it. He doesn't need them down here. It's pitch black."

"Oh." Neil remembered standing in the black, liquid void before Elden had arrived.

Off in the distance, Neil saw a parade of white and blue, bioluminescent jellyfish floating through the water. He watched as they sailed slowly through the current.

As he rose higher in the ocean, Neil heard humpback whales singing to each other. He tried to imitate their sounds; but Elden asked him to stop.

"You might confuse them or call too much attention to us."

Purple fish, midnight blue across the tops of their slender bodies, looked at Neil and Elden as they swam by. They wore faint gold lines on their heads and spots of gold on their bodies, as though dressed for show.

A bright orange fish, round like a circle, with short stubby fins decorated with an orange and white mosaic pattern, swam toward the boy and the dolphin. It stared at them with big black eyes and then changed direction.

Neil giggled in spite of himself when a small group of yellow seahorses swam in front of them. He imagined the seahorses taking part in a race. Elden swerved to the left to avoid them.

Then they broke through the water. The full moon illuminated the long, curling whitecaps as they rose and fell and ran toward the beach. The pounding surf echoed against the black wall of night. Stars glowed like electric sand thrown across the sky.

Neil held tightly onto Elden's back fin as the waves jostled against them.

"Neil, I'm going to take you as far into shore as I can. I'll watch you swim the rest of the way."

Neil looked at the rolling, menacing whitecaps.

"You'll be fine. Now, I need for you to remember something important." Elden paused. "Do you want to see your mother again?"

"Yes!"

"Then you need to tell Wiley and Keegan to meet me at the beach after sunrise. Tell them to bring all the boys, including you. Tell them that Keegan must hold the golden cup under the water. Tell them that I will see the cup, and that I will then take all of you back to your city under the ocean."

Neil climbed off Elden's back and wrapped his arms, as far as he could reach, around Elden's neck. He hugged him as tightly as he could.

"Thank you, Elden. Thank you."

CHAPTER 14

Nevin woke up in the early morning. The sun had only begun, with broad brushstrokes, to paint brilliant pinks and oranges and dusty red upon the midnight blue sky. The sun itself was a molten sphere of orange and yellow lava burning through the clouds at the far horizon.

Birds sang in the darkish green trees of the forest. The surf pounded against the shore. The smell of seaweed and salt and fish hung in the air.

Nevin rolled over in his warm fleece blanket cocoon. Realizing suddenly where he was, he opened his eyes to see if Neil was sleeping.

He was gone!

Charged with fear, Nevin woke completely and jumped to his feet. He started yelling and running from boy to boy, in a desperate attempt to wake everyone at once. Calder moaned. Not comprehending Nevin's words, he rolled over and went back to sleep. Everyone else sat up and rubbed their eyes.

"He's gone! Just gone!"

Arthur spoke next, "If you're pulling one of your practical jokes, Nevin, I'm not going to be amused at this early hour!"

"I'm not!"

Keegan spoke next, “Look at him, Arthur. You can tell he’s not joking.”

“Oh, my word!” Nevin froze for a moment as he looked toward the ocean. The other boys followed the direction of his gaze. On the sand a few feet from where the water was now sliding onto land was a small boy wrapped in brownish green seaweed.

Nevin moved slowly toward the seaweed as though swimming through liquid. He did not want to see what he thought was there. When he reached the body, he saw the long, golden curls of hair that he knew so well spread out on the sand, saturated with sand and salt and water. Greenish brown, slimy seaweed had wrapped itself around the body and crawled into the hair.

Nevin bent down and rolled the body from its side to its back, so that he could get a good look at the face. In the moment that he realized it was indeed his little brother, a sigh came from the seaweed. Then words.

“I’m tired! Let me sleep!”

Nevin paused, then jumped to his feet.

“Neil, what do you think you’re doing? How could you leave camp? You know better! You don’t go down to the ocean by yourself! And you never go into the water at night!”

No response from Neil.

“Neil, wake up! You need to explain to me what you were thinking! When did you leave camp?”

Neil rolled from his back onto his side. His teeth chattered with cold; he pulled his knees up to his chest and tried to pull the seaweed closer like a blanket. He was sorely disappointed with the thick, gelatinous substance that left slime and grit in the palms of his hands.

Wiley spoke next, "Nevin, you need to warm him up. Carry him back to the blankets. Wrap him up. I'll start a fire and we'll heat some apple juice."

"No, he'll talk to me first!"

Wiley pulled Nevin aside by the arm and spoke to him more quietly, "Nevin, I know you're worried about Neil. But if you don't warm him up soon, you may lose him. He's very cold. I've seen this with fishermen on the island. It's dangerous to get that cold."

Nevin kicked sand in a direction away from the pile that was his brother. He stared angrily at the deep blue clouds now filling with explosions of color along the horizon.

Then he bent down and picked up the cold, slippery mass that was his brother. As he did so, he noticed that Neil's face was ashen white and that his teeth were clacking rapidly against each other.

"Don't worry, Neil. Everything will be all right. We'll take good care of you."

Nevin, holding his brother, ran from the beach where he had found him to the place where the boys had set up camp the night before.

Wiley ran ahead of them. When he reached the burned out campfire, he threw himself to his knees in the sand. He reached under a nearby blanket where he had kept sticks and blankets dry from the wet night air. He threw the wood into the pile of old ashes and lit the timber with a match from his pants pocket.

Arthur spread one blanket open on the sand near the growing fire. He told Nevin to place his brother on the blanket. Nevin placed him there, removed as much seaweed as he could quickly remove from his brother's cold skin, and then wrapped him in every blanket he could find.

Wiley found a pot and a container of apple juice. As he heated the sweet substance, the aroma smelled like apple pie that reminded the boys how hungry they were. Before the liquid bubbled, as soon as steam rose like morning mist from the pot, Wiley poured the juice into a tin cup.

As he sipped the warm, steaming liquid, pinkish color crept slowly into Neil's cheeks and lips. His teeth stopped chattering. Slowly, he looked around at the other boys. He looked up at Nevin.

"I'm sorry."

Nevin bit his lower lip and fought back tears. "You better be! You'd better not ever do that again!"

Neil looked away from his brother's fierce eyes toward the increasingly light blue sky along the horizon.

"I met with the dolphin last night."

"That's nice."

Wiley, who had been listening as he prepared a breakfast of hot porridge over the campfire, paused. “What did you say, Neil?”

“Last night I met with the dolphin.”

“What dolphin? What do you mean?”

“You know, the dolphin who brought us here on his back.”

“Elden?”

“I guess that’s his name.”

Nevin interrupted, “You were dreaming, Neil.”

“No, I wasn’t. I rode on his back down to our city. I saw Mother and Father … And I saw my friends: Garrett, and Jackson, and Rafferty. Rafferty taught me this great way to build toy walls with dice to protect toy soldiers. And I saw Aunt Chloe, and Julian, and Helen. They stayed for lunch. Mother made this incredible meal…”

“Neil, stop it!”

Tears flooded Nevin’s eyes, broke the dam and spilled down his cheeks. He wiped them away with the back of his hand and stomped away toward the place where he had found Neil. He kicked seashells that he found along the way.

Wiley picked up the conversation where Nevin had ended it.

“Did Elden mention anything about the goblet?”

Neil looked up with wide eyes. “Yes. He said that we should all go down to the ocean, that you and Keegan should bring all of us there. Keegan should place the golden goblet under the water. He said that we should do that today, after sunrise, and that he will bring us down to our city. He said that I can see my Mother!"

"All right. Let's have breakfast. Then we leave for the ocean."

As the boys ate steaming bowls of porridge and drank warmed cups of apple juice, Wiley told them what Neil had said. Kingston and Nevin snickered quietly under their breath.

Wiley turned toward each boy, one at a time. "Let's go down to the ocean. Let's just see what happens."

Keegan spoke for everyone when he said, "There's no harm in that."

The boys cleaned up breakfast dishes, folded blankets, and put out the fire. They hid all of their belongings in a wooded area next to the path they had taken to the beach. Then they went down to the water. At Wiley's insistence, they all waded into the ocean and Keegan placed the golden goblet under the water.

Within moments, a large marine animal swam close by, slapping the boys one by one with its tail. The boys shrieked; then watched as Elden rose from the water, and danced backward on the waves. He appeared to be smiling.

Suddenly, a beluga whale burst from the water and breached above the waves.

"Beluga!" Wiley grinned and shouted and waved. "Beluga! Elden!" Wiley turned to Neil. "You're going home, Neil! You're going home to see your parents!"

Then Wiley looked at Keegan and shrugged his shoulders. Had Neil truly swam with Elden the night before and been told how the boys should contact the dolphin?

Keegan shrugged his shoulders back. Then he looked around him. In the distance, two more dolphins leapt into the air and returned to the water. Then they disappeared for a time.

Moments later, the dolphins' heads emerged from the water near Elden.

Elden spoke without words. "We want to give you all a comfortable ride down to the ancient city. These are my friends, Gladwin and Colt. They've come to help us. Nevin, you ride with your brother on Colt's back."

Nevin lifted Neil up. Water splashed from his feet, sprayed in circular directions and filled with tiny rainbows, as Neil rose above the water and landed gently on Colt's back. Nevin climbed up behind his brother. He wrapped one arm around Neil and used his other hand to hold onto Colt's top fin.

Elden communicated to Wiley as he had done so many times before, "Wiley, climb up on my back." Then he addressed the other boys, "Keegan, you ride on Beluga. Arthur, climb up behind Keegan. And, Kingston and Calder, hop up onto Gladwin."

As soon as the boys had followed his directions, Elden dipped below the surface to lead the caravan on its quest for the old city, the place that had been named in ancient times, "The City of the Golden Sun."

Wiley saw so much that had become familiar to him.

He watched the sandy bottom where seaweed grew in abundance as he and Elden glided above it. He smiled as a school of black-and-white striped fish with a splash of yellow on their backs swam into the midst of the caravan. These fish were brave, thought Wiley, considering their small size.

Wiley heard Neil giggle as a fish in full costume swam by. It had spiked fins, transparent with a greenish tint for the most part, but more solid in white and orange color closer to the body at the base of the fins. The body itself was black-and-white striped. The head of the fish was bright orange with a large black spot on either side. The fish had red eyes surrounded by a bulging white bubble.

Neil laughed so hard, Wiley was afraid he might fall off Colt's back.

Kingston's heart pounded as something he thought was a rock moved at the bottom of the ocean. It was the color and texture of sand. As it pulled itself from a burrow it had made on the ocean floor, Kingston saw that it had green eyes.

After traveling for awhile, the boys observed a sudden drop in the ocean floor. Like arriving at the edge of a canyon, the boys suddenly arrived at a precipice. Beluga and the dolphins pointed their noses straight downward and took the boys deeper.

Sunlight faded. Temperature cooled and chilled. The boys adjusted. Their vision gradually cleared and their bodies warmed.

The boys watched in silence as a wall of jellyfish came alive and floated toward them. Each jelly, a perfectly rounded gossamer dome of glowing pastels and translucent white, floated toward them and past them.

As they descended further, Neil shivered and cried, "The water is too heavy! Ow! The water hurts!"

Nevin spoke to his brother, "Come on, Neil. You're fine."

Elden interrupted him. "This may be uncomfortable for Neil because he's small. He'll adjust; but it will be difficult."

Elden turned his head toward Beluga. "Keegan, do you still have the golden cup?"

"Yes."

"Then give it to Neil. It will remind him of home, and the blue gemstones will protect him against the weight and cold of the water."

Keegan pulled the golden goblet from beneath his shirt. Beluga swam over to Colt. Keegan extended his arm, so that Neil could grab the goblet. Nevin grabbed it for him and handed it to his younger brother.

"Now, don't lose this, Neil, or you're going to be in serious trouble. That's my guess. We're going deeper and you're having difficulties at this level."

Neil's teeth chattered and clacked against each other. "I won't, Nevin! Stop picking on me!"

Nevin rolled his eyes upward in annoyance. He was startled to see complete darkness, like a black ceiling, as he did so.

Up ahead, small clouds of glowing purple illuminated the midnight blackness, creating small pockets of light.

Kingston was the first to speak, “What’s that?”

Beluga answered, “Look closer.”

The boys stared and strained to make out shapes. Kingston noticed first the silver shapes resembling snakes with spikes of hair and large eyes. Wiley recognized the creatures from fishermen’s lore. “Squid. Those are squid.”

Beluga responded, “Right! Down here, some squid produce ink that glows in the dark.”

Neil’s eyes widened with excitement. “Really?”

“Yes. How do you like that?”

“I’d like to have some of that ink!”

Nevin laughed. Beluga’s smile widened.

The caravan continued onward. From somewhere far off in the distance, the songs of humpback whales permeated the depths. The boys found the groaning music strangely comforting.

At some point, everyone in the caravan became aware of a huge amount of glowing light: red, orange, yellow. Wiley imagined the giant squid of the fishermen’s stories. Neil wrapped his arms around Colt’s neck. Nevin held on more tightly to Neil.

As the caravan descended to the ocean floor, the boys saw a large beast.

Wiley's heart pounded wildly in his chest, like a caged animal trying to escape. "Elden, that's the Fire Beast. I killed him!"

"It's not really the Fire Beast. It's a memory. Something that strong and powerful clings to time and reality even after its demise. We're about to travel through time. As time bends and warps, it sometimes doubles back on itself and drags part of the past into the present. Think of it like a ribbon blowing in the breeze. It moves backwards and forwards. So, too, with time. It bends and twists."

As Elden spoke, the caravan witnessed Wiley as he defeated the Beast. Wiley saw himself in action, riding into battle on Beluga's back. Clutching the golden sword, swimming through the deafening roar and blazing fire, Wiley reached the Beast. Wiley drove the sword hard into its stomach. Purple blood poured from its wound and dyed the boiling water with its color.

Elden spoke firmly, "Listen to me. You will not remember this until later. You will know only that you live within The City of the Golden Sun. Wiley, you are a servant within Keegan's household. You are treated well there. You were taken in when your father, a fisherman, lost his life at sea. Best of luck. I'll be back later."

The boys were thrown from the backs of Elden, Beluga, Colt and Gladwin. The water swirled purple, then rushed straight up into the heavens and disappeared.

Part II

In The City of the Golden Sun

Around the 5th century B.C.

CHAPTER 15

Wiley woke up as he had done every day for as far back as he could remember - in the servants' quarters of the palace. The King was very kind. The servants' quarters were comfortable. They were located next door to the palace itself. The servants' building was constructed from white marble, the same as the palace. It was simply smaller and less ornate.

Within the servants' building, there were apartments for families and single rooms for servants without families. Wiley lived in a single room. He had vague memories of fishing at sea with his father, vague memories of his father's face; but that was about it. He didn't even clearly remember when he had received the news that his father had died at sea. He just remembered the shock of the news.

Then he remembered coming to live at the palace. The King had been looking for someone to help with the care of the horses. Wiley had always been good with animals. Calder had recommended him to Keegan, and Keegan had suggested him to his father. His father, the King, had agreed to give him a chance.

Wiley had done wonderfully, cleaning out the stalls, feeding, grooming, and giving water to the horses. He had also become great friends with

Keegan, spending time with him when the young prince came to ride his horse.

Keegan's father was liberal, indulgent with his son, and kind. He did not object to Keegan spending time with servant children if they were decent children; and he did not expect any child, servant or not, to work all day. He supplied all of the palace help with good food, pleasant living conditions, and free time. He deemed education and playtime important for all children, whether rich or poor.

Wiley had become best friends with Keegan.

On this particular day, Keegan stood outside Wiley's window and whistled with his fingers in his mouth until Wiley opened his bedroom window.

"Keegan, you're going to wake everyone up."

"No, everyone's already awake. Get ready! The Festival is today!"

CHAPTER 16

Kingston had been up before dawn. The sky had been black and cool. The moon, not yet worn out, had spilled moonlight onto Kingston's bedroom floor so that he could find his way out of bed.

Kingston's father had woken him early. "Come on, Kingston, get up. I have to leave for the theatre." His father watched him closely for any sign of movement. "Come on, Kingston! I'm leaving."

"I hear you. I hear you." Kingston covered his head with his pillow.

His father removed the pillow.

"Come on. I have to make sure you're up. Today is the day of the Festival of the Sun. I don't want you to miss it."

Kingston opened one eye, then shut it. "Today?"

"Yes. Come on! Get up!"

Kingston removed his blankets, swung his feet over the side of the bed, and rubbed his eyes. "All right. I'm up."

Kingston's father looked annoyed even in the half-light. "All the way up. Come on. I want to see that you're awake. Come downstairs. There's hot cereal on the table."

Kingston stood up and followed his father downstairs. His father looked much like him, but older: thick, dark brown hair, deep brown eyes, and ruddy cheeks. Like his son, Thaddeus Ivers had a strong, emotional personality. Since losing his wife and Kingston's mother in an accident three years earlier, he had found it more difficult to stay calm. The theatre was a great refuge. He was an actor.

Today was the annual Festival of the Sun, a day-long celebration of theatre, song, parades, and feasting. Kingston's father patted him on the head as he sat down to his breakfast. "Bye, son. Is Nevin's family definitely stopping by for you?"

"Yes. Definitely."

"Well, see you at the Festival then. Remember, I'm in the first play, and then in two others during the day."

Thaddeus wrapped a gray toga around himself, opened the door and stepped outside.

Kingston turned to his hot cereal and the silence in the room. He tried to hurry, so that he wouldn't miss the parade that started on one side of the city and ended at the theatre on the other.

Then he realized that he had time. The sun was not yet up.

CHAPTER 17

Calder woke up in the middle of the night. He threw back his covers, and crossed his wooden bedroom floor in bare feet to open his window. Sticking his head outside, he let the cool air and moonlight wash over him.

The stars burned brightly. His small backyard was filled with trees and shadows and bright, moonlit patches of green. He could barely make out the small, square vegetable garden in the far right corner next to the stone wall.

Today was the day. He would march in the procession across town, singing and cheering. He would watch one play after another with no book lessons to interrupt him. He would eat wonderful food at the feasts. He would see his friends.

More than anything else, Calder Torannen wanted to be an actor when he grew up. More than anything else today, he wanted to watch the plays and speak with the actors.

When would the moon go to bed and let the sun spread its banners across the sky, letting everyone know that this was the day and that it could officially begin?

CHAPTER 18

Nevin and Neil's mother walked into their separate bedrooms and woke them up. In each of the rooms, she opened the window shutters so that the sun splashed across her sons' faces and roused them from sleep.

"Good morning. Today is the Festival of the Sun! Wake up. Breakfast is on the table."

Nevin rubbed his eyes, rolled over for a few moments and then slowly removed himself from his bed. The instant that Neil recognized what day this was, he bolted out of bed, jumped up and down a few times, and ran into the kitchen. He hugged his mother and sat down at the table.

In between mouthfuls of warm bread smothered in honey, Neil talked with his mother about the Festival.

"Is my costume ready?"

"What do you think?"

Neil parted his sticky lips and smiled. "It's ready?"

"Yes."

"Oh, good! I can't wait!"

Neil jumped off his chair, ran around the table two times, and sat back down again just as his older brother entered the kitchen.

"Nevin, my costume's ready!" Neil paused for a moment. "Is Nevin's ready? Is it finished?"

Neil's mother carried a ceramic pitcher of grape juice over to the table and set it down. "What do you think?"

"Yes?"

"Yes, it's ready."

Nevin pulled a generously large piece from the circular loaf of warm bread resting on a plate in the middle of the table. He placed it on a smaller plate and poured honey from a small pitcher onto his dish. He paused briefly to thank his mother. Then he alternated dipping the bread into the honey and shoving the bread into his mouth, chewing ravenously with each mouthful.

"This is delicious!"

"It's from the MacFinnbhair's bakery."

"I thought it tasted familiar! This is my favorite bread!"

Nevin's mother smiled as she poured more grape juice into Neil's now empty cup. She spoke to Nevin, "If you need more juice, let me know."

"I will. Thanks."

When Neil had had his fill, he jumped down off his chair.

"Can I have my costume now? Can I? Where is it?"

"Whoa! Hold on! I don't want that honey on your costume!"

Neil reached up with his hands and felt around his mouth. "Oh. Honey."

Neil's mother grimaced. "Now it's all over your hands, too."

"It already was."

"Well, come here."

Neil's mother wiped his hands and face with a warm, wet cloth. Then she told him to wait in his bedroom.

Neil jumped up and down on his bed until his mother entered the room with a costume draped over her arm. When she unfolded it and held it up, Neil could see that it was the costume of a bear.

"I love it! I'll be the fiercest, meanest bear ever! Can I put it on?"

"You can put it on if you don't go near the kitchen table. I don't want any honey or juice on it!"

"But bears like honey!"

"I mean it, Neil."

"I was just being funny. I'm done eating. I can't wait for the parade!"

"Well, get dressed then. I'll be in the kitchen."

When Nevin finished his breakfast, he washed up and asked for his costume.

"I put it on your bed."

The Festival of the Sun was an annual summer holiday to celebrate life flourishing in the sun. It was an all-day affair involving a parade from one side of the city to another, theatre plays, singing, dancing, and banquet-sized tables filled with every imaginable kind of food. In the parade, all of the adults wore something yellow to symbolize the sun. All of the children wore costumes of plants and animals that thrive under the guidance of the sun.

Neil emerged from his room dressed like a bear. He sneaked up behind his mother and raised his arms. "Roar!"

Neil's mother shrieked in pretend fright and then hugged her youngest son. "You'll be great today!"

Nevin sneaked quietly from his room to just behind Neil. "Roar!"

Neil jumped and screamed in real, momentary fright. Then he chased his older brother around the table until their mother told them to stop. "Save that energy for the parade!"

CHAPTER 19

The crowd gathered on the outskirts of the city on a small hill. From a distance, one could see splashes of yellow throughout the gathering and small animals running about. There was a buzz, a hum, and great chaotic movement. Color waved in the breeze like flowers on a windy day.

Then there arose the sound of trumpets. Song followed, invading the small mountain and floating above the city. The milling crowd condensed itself into a line four people across. Adults who knew the words chanted the answers to the words of the professional singers.

"We flourish in the sun. We grow. We blossom. There's life for everyone."

"We dance. We sing. Today we are alive."

Wiley rubbed his left hand on the opposite sleeve of his owl costume. He couldn't believe how much he looked like an owl. He looked at Keegan, dressed like a dolphin. Something about the dolphin costume stirred up feelings deep within him; but he couldn't place his finger on the memory.

What was it? It made him feel both happy and scared at the same time. He assumed it was a memory from a fishing expedition with his father. Maybe something had gone wrong. As he attempted to retrieve the memory, he was caught up in the excitement of the crowd and forgot about it a few seconds later.

"We dance. We sing. Today we are alive."

As the crowd descended from the hill, the front lines reached the edges of an outlying neighborhood. Keegan's father, King Reginauld, was waiting there in a golden chariot pulled by large, muscular horses. Sun reflected from the golden chariot and the deep black sheen of the horses' hair.

Surrounding the King's chariot were soldiers on horseback. They wore short linen tunics, silver metal plates over their arms, legs, and chests, and silver metal helmets. They waved large, decorative shields and swords above their heads as the crowd approached.

Sunlight danced from the swords and shields in riotous confusion. The crowd shouted and cheered.

The trumpets blasted again and the crowd burst into song.

"We dance beneath the sun. We swim and roar and crawl."

"We are the animals. Today we are alive!"

Neil reached up and tapped Nevin on the arm as they marched along.

"We're animals, Nevin! We're bears!"

"What?"

"We're animals! We're bears!"

Nevin strained to hear his little brother over the roar of the crowd. "What?"

Neil lifted up his mask. "We're bears, Nevin! We're animals!"

"Oh, I know! Isn't this fun?"

Neil smiled and returned his mask to his face. "Roar! Roar! I'm a bear!"

CHAPTER 20

As the processional for the Festival of the Sun flowed down the hill, Wiley drank in the view of the city. It was basically a circular city that had grown up inside a rectangular barrier. The walls that surrounded the city were made from multi-colored rock. On top of the walls were long, rectangular boxes filled with brightly colored flowers. At the main entrance to the city was a gate made of thin, golden bars topped with a golden arch. Thousands of gemstones in a multitude of colors decorated the gate. Set into the arch were the words: " Drink deeply by land or sea. Earth comes only once."

Wiley thought about how the people of this city really did drink deeply by land or sea. They loved life, celebrated life, and deeply enjoyed all the benefits of their culture. They had plays in the center of town. They had beautiful buildings. Running water came into the homes through a system of aqueducts and pipes. They had bakeries and restaurants bustling with customers. Jewelry, pottery, and metal goblets were for sale in the markets. Life was rich and full.

As the procession moved down the hill, Wiley observed that, inside the walls, an expanse of rich green hills surrounded the city. At the base of the hills, the outskirts of the city were made from a dense collection of houses and apartments. Most of the roofs were red, covered in terracotta tiles. From up above the city, the houses looked to Wiley like a giant's collection of red dice. In the very center of the city stood the huge white marble buildings: the temples, government buildings, a stadium with a racetrack, libraries. Slightly off to the right was the palace and its related buildings, including the building where Wiley lived.

Directly across from the hill where the procession began, on the opposite hill, was the largest theatre in the city. Throughout the day, plays would be brought to life on the stage there. Wiley intended to visit there, at least for a part of the day.

"Wiley, look I'm a flower."

Wiley looked behind him. It was Nevin and Neil's cousin, Helen. She was covered in pieces of yellow cloth, each one in the shape of a flower petal. As Wiley watched, Helen's brother, Julian, came up behind her and raised his arms. Then he threw his arms around her.

"Yes, and I'm a rabbit. I'm going to eat you!"

Helen shrieked, and ran in circles as soon as her brother let go. Julian chased her in and out of the people nearby until their mother told them in a stern voice to stop.

The procession continued down the hill.

As he reached the edge of the city, Wiley stepped onto a cobblestone road. He ran ahead to join the section directly behind the group of royalty at the head of the parade. He heard the golden chariot carrying the King moving forward on the cobblestone road, the clack of the horses' hooves and the movement of the large wheels as they spun 'round-and-'round.

On the parade route, Wiley passed by rows of houses, apartments, and small shops. Most were made from gray and white stone and had brightly colored curtains in the windows. Many had box windowsills filled with flowers.

When he reached the center of town, Wiley noticed that huge tables had been set up on both sides of the main road to sell food and wares. The scent of freshly roasted meat, rich, bubbling stew and warm, baking bread floated on the wind to greet him.

Wiley decided to ignore his sudden hunger pangs and search for his friends. Keegan would stay with his father and move ahead to the chariot races in the stadium. Most of Wiley's other friends would march ahead to the theatre.

Nevin and Neil's parents would go to the theatre to support the actors who practiced in their bookshop. Kingston would go there to watch his father perform. Calder would attend because he loved the theatre and hoped someday to be an actor. Keegan would show up later at the theatre when his father, the King, attended a play.

The only friend he wasn't sure about was Arthur. Arthur could be anywhere.

When the crowd reached the main street, people were free to go wherever they wanted. A large procession led by the royal family continued on to the stadium. The remainder of the crowd dispersed to other locations.

Wiley walked down the main street. He listened to his shoes clap against the cobblestones. He looked from side to side at all the tables. Drawn to a table of toys, he walked over to inspect it more closely. There were armies of terracotta soldiers, piles of knucklebones and dice, rag dolls, board games, and marbles. And a gold-plated toy chariot, the most beautiful toy Wiley had ever seen. An exact replica of the King's chariot, it glistened in the sun.

"Hey, boy, what are you looking at?"

A rough-looking man in a gray tunic stood up on the other side of the table, placed his open hands on the surface, and leaned in toward Wiley. He had coarse black stubble on his face, chapped lips and bloodshot eyes. He glared at Wiley.

"You're not going to steal it, are you?"

Wiley looked at the man with widened eyes. "Of course not. I'm just looking." After an uncomfortable silence, Wiley added, "My friend's father owns that chariot. I've ridden in it a few times."

The man let out a deep, rumbling laugh that echoed off the cobblestone road. "Ha! Sure! Sure, you have!" Then he leaned in even more closely to Wiley, as his face contorted from smiling to grimacing. Deep, wrinkled lines changed position on the man's weatherworn face. "That's the King's chariot! Get away from here, you lying thief!"

Wiley jumped backward away from the table and headed back down the street. He decided to continue his trek to the theatre. Later in the day, he hoped to see at least one or two chariot races in the stadium. But, first, he wanted to find his friends.

Wiley walked through a maze of large, marble buildings. He passed by one of his favorites, the Temple of the Sun. Then he stopped suddenly and went back. He had free time today and could spend some time investigating quietly on his own.

He looked at the large front porch lined with a front and back row of tall, white marble columns. He ran up the six wide marble steps that led to the porch. Then he let himself go, running in and out of the columns, listening to the echo of his shoes on the cool marble floor.

When he tired of running, Wiley walked over to the center door. There were five golden doors that reached from the floor to the porch roof. Wiley pulled the golden door handle intricately carved to look like a lion's tail and walked inside.

The quiet enveloped Wiley. In the center of the room was a statue of a former King, easily seven times the height of a full-grown man. In one outstretched hand, he held a golden ball representing the sun. In the other hand, he held a white crystal. This was King Roarke, credited with the discovery of the Sun Crystal, the largest, most powerful crystal in the entire city. The statue was made from gold and decorated with a multitude of sparkling gemstones.

Wiley laid down on one of the wooden benches that ran along the walls of the room. He turned partially on his left side and observed how daylight poured through the sky roof and bounced off the large crystal and the smaller gemstones. As quiet fell upon him like a soft blanket, Wiley noticed rainbows splashed and dancing throughout the room. Like sunlight on a pond, the rainbows changed position, enlivening the plain white walls.

After watching the dancing rainbows for a considerable amount of time, Wiley sat up, jumped off the bench, and ran outside. Hurtling two steps at a time, he landed back on the road.

Wiley traveled across the city and trudged up the hill to the large theatre. He noticed that people had already filled most of the audience seats in the semicircular outdoor room. There was a hum and buzz from the crowd as they waited for the first performance.

Climbing up the steep hill, Wiley had his face turned toward the ground when he heard Nevin and Kingston calling his name. He looked up to see Nevin, Kingston, and Calder running toward him. They were smiling broadly. Calder was waving his hands and arms wildly, trying to attract his attention.

Wiley stopped and planted his feet firmly on the sloping hill. "What are you all doing?"

"We're going to the chariot races! We were hoping to find you!"

"What? What about the theatre?"

Kingston answered, "The first play of the day is for grown-ups only."

Nevin interrupted, "My Aunt is watching Neil. The rest of us are free to go our own way."

Calder spoke next, "In the afternoon, there are two plays for children. We're free all morning."

"Woooo weeeee! Let's go!" Wiley could hardly contain his excitement, thinking about the slick black chariot, the yellow chariot, the shiny red chariot, the muscular, snorting horses, the clouds of dust on the racetrack, the sweet drinks and cakes in the stadium. "Let's go! Let's go! What are you waiting for?"

Kingston echoed Wiley's excitement, "Woooo weeeee!"

The boys ran down the grassy hill. Calder tripped over a rock and rolled down the slope. He burst into laughter as he came finally to a stop. "Ha! That was fun!" He jumped to his feet. "Let's go!"

The boys ran as far as the middle of town, then slowed down. Calder bent over and held his stomach. Breathlessly, he said to the other boys, "That's it for me. I walk the rest of the way."

Kingston and Wiley responded at the same time, "That's fine with me."

As the boys walked along the main road, they looked from side to side at the long tables.

Calder asked his friends, "Do you want to get something to eat?"

Wiley answered quickly, "Why don't we get food in the stadium? That's so much fun!"

"Oh, I forgot. Let's get food there first. We can have a bigger meal later."

The boys continued on toward the stadium. As they passed by a small white marble sanctuary with a red terracotta roof, someone yelled to them, "Boys!"

Wiley answered first, "Who's that?"

"Arthur! Come here! Behind the building!"

The boys walked slowly toward the back of the building, glancing around as they went. When Wiley who was first in line reached the back of the building, someone grabbed him by the arm.

"Don't scream!"

Wiley found himself looking directly into Arthur's face, into his serious blue eyes. Thick black eyebrows, pulled into two small arches, extended from his wrinkled forehead.

"Arthur, what's wrong?"

"I need all of you to come with me. You absolutely will not believe what I found if you don't see it for yourselves."

Nevin was the first to complain, "What about the chariot races? We had permission to go there all morning!"

"You won't mind missing them when I show you what I've found."

Wiley spoke next, "Like what? What is it?"

"I can't tell you here." Arthur looked all around, as though watching for someone. "Just come with me to the mines. You can leave if you aren't interested."

Again, Wiley spoke up, "To the mines? Are you crazy? That's outside the city! We'll lose a lot of our festival time! Let's do it tomorrow."

Arthur grabbed Wiley again by the arm. "No, we can't do it tomorrow. What I've got to show you won't wait until tomorrow."

CHAPTER 21

The boys passed through the back gate leading from the main city into the mines. The mining area was contained within its own rock walls; but the walls here did not have flower boxes running along the top.

On the other side of the mines was a village, named by its people simply "The Village by the Sea." It was laid out within another large rectangle of rock walls. Despite the close location, the two properties did not mingle very much other than to trade products. Keegan's city produced artwork, books, plays, and jewelry. It also had a large fishing industry and produced marble. The village next-door was more agricultural, raising wheat, oats, fruit, cows, goats, and sheep.

Both places shared a gold mine, with the back gate of each city opening into the mining area. The front gate of each property faced toward the ocean on opposite sides of the island. The front gate to Wiley's city saw sunrise. The front gate to the farming village saw sunset.

The relationship between the two properties was fragile. The citizens in Keegan's city enjoyed great freedom. People were encouraged to participate in the arts and to think for themselves. Most of the servants were treated well and allowed free time.

On the other side of the mines, life was harder. People began their days at sunrise and did not quit until after sunset. With all of the hard work that needed to be done on the farms, people did not have time for the arts or entertainment. Servants were treated like slaves, as they were expected to work harder than their masters.

Due to their differences, wars between the two locations were common until gold was discovered beneath the ground on the land that ran between the two back gates. Most likely, the people would have fought over the mines as well, except that both properties were now in danger of being attacked for their gold by outside countries. Therefore, they needed to stick together in order to protect the island itself.

Both the city and the village traded with another island for silver, pearls, horses, and lightweight wood. Unfortunately, people on that other island were known for their aggression and for their tendency to conquer civilizations they deemed important to their growth. Now that Keegan's island had discovered gold, there was nervousness about possible invasion.

Arthur grabbed Wiley by the arm, held on with his right hand, and pointed straight ahead with his left. Almost under his breath, he said, "Look."

The boys looked straight ahead at the mine. Keegan squinted in order to block out the sun. "What's happening?"

"You don't get it?"

Wiley gasped. "What's going on? Official orders were given for no one to work the mines today because of the Festival of the Sun. The village on the other side agreed not to work the mines today!"

"Look closer. That's our men."

"Oh …" For a moment, Wiley was speechless. "What do they think they're doing? That's too dangerous - mining after asking the village not to touch the gold!"

Arthur waved his hand in order to direct his friends to an area behind a cluster of trees. The boys walked into the sheltered area. They continued to peer out from behind the thick brush.

Keegan saw it first. He pointed toward the harbor for the neighboring village. In an unmistakably agitated voice, he asked, "What's that?"

Calder was the first to answer, "A ship! Whose sails are those?"

The boys studied the ship. It was huge. Made from dark wood with ornate carvings along the railings, and a huge carved wooden dragon on the front. The dragon had been painted green with red, orange and yellow fire billowing from its mouth. On either side of the ship, toward the front, a blue eye had been painted, ever watchful, the warriors' hope for protection. A massive sail curved outward as the wind gave it life and blew the ship swiftly toward shore. The white sail swelled, revealing a large black X with a red star in its center.

"That ship is from the island we trade with!"

Kingston interrupted him, "But it's a war ship!"

Arthur noticed the teams of men rowing the vessel. "Why are they coming here?"

Wiley looked behind him at the feasting and celebrating city. The noise of celebration drowned out all noise from the approaching boat. "Should we tell the men in the mines?"

Kingston was the first to answer, "No! They'll start yelling at us and call attention to themselves from the men sailing in on that ship."

Calder spoke next, "If the men coming in on that ship have bad intentions, the men in the mine will know about it soon."

Suddenly, Wiley ran from behind a tree and hid behind another one closer to the edge of the thicket. He pointed. "Look! Look over there! What is that?"

Calder answered him, "It's a light! It's blindingly bright! But where is it coming from? What is it?"

The boys searched the landscape for a clue. Nevin saw it first. "Look over there! Look! Look! What is that?"

On a mountain slope rising above the village was a huge object, a mirror shaped like a bowl on a moving stand. The bowl was standing on its side, with the bottom center of the bowl facing toward the approaching ship. The sun's rays poured into the mirror bowl like streams of glowing hot liquid. Focused, the sun reflected outward toward the ship. As the boys watched, the sail ignited. The red star lit up brilliantly; then turned to ash floating on the wind. Shortly after that, the entire ship exploded into flames.

The men in the mine kept working, hearing only the noise from the Festival.

CHAPTER 22

Keegan spoke in a hurried voice, "We need to get out of here, fast! Before the men in the mine or the people at the Festival see the smoke from the ship! Come on! Let's go!"

The boys ran, as one closely-knit group, in the shape of a large moving knot, one minute untying, the next minute tying itself more tightly. Suddenly, Arthur ran ahead, his long black hair bouncing up and down on his back and flying out behind him. "I'll open the gate! Hurry!"

Arthur opened the gate. One by one, the boys ran through it, back into their own city. Out of breath, the boys stopped on the inner side of the gate. Calder bent forward at the waist, breathing heavily, waiting for his heart to slow down.

Arthur passed through the entrance after his friends had gone through. He looked at them with glistening, widened eyes. "We can't stop here! We'll get caught!"

The boys looked blankly at Arthur.

"As soon as they see the smoke, the men from the mines are going to run through this gate! Come on!"

Nevin spoke next, "Why would that be a problem? We're allowed near the city gates, you know."

"But why would we be here? With the Festival going on, why would we be standing around the back gate? The men will get suspicious and ask questions. Let's go!"

Keegan responded, "You're right. But, think about it, we always walk from place to place, exploring at the Festival. Let's just start walking to something. We don't need to run."

Wiley made the next suggestion, "Let's go to the stadium! I wanted to see the chariot races anyway, and it's nearby!"

Keegan and Arthur answered together, "Yes!"

Keegan continued, "Let's go find my father. He's at the stadium. We'll sit with the King and we'll be fine."

Agreeing that that was a great idea, the boys started walking along the cobblestone road, away from the gate that led to the mines. Slowly, they regained their breath.

After they had put some distance between themselves and the gate, Arthur turned around, placed his right hand over his eyes in order to shield them from the sun, and scanned the sky over the village harbor. It was filled with a large, black cloud of smoke.

"I don't understand it. That cloud is so visible. But our men haven't returned from the mines."

Nevin responded to Arthur's observation, "Should we tell someone about what we saw? Do you think the men are in danger?"

"I don't know. I don't think they're in immediate danger. The other village was being invaded."

Before Arthur could express all of what he was thinking, Keegan interrupted him, "Unless we're next. Are we being invaded, too?" Keegan's heart pounded in his chest and fluttered wildly, like a fish caught in a net. "We need to tell someone."

"All right. Let's do what we were going to do. Let's join your father at the stadium. Let's see what happens. If no one mentions the invasion, we'll tell your father."

"Good. But let's hurry! I don't know how much time we have left!"

CHAPTER 23

The boys, led by Keegan, approached the stadium. The closer they got, the louder the roar from the crowd. Keegan had a sinking feeling within his heart. The crowd didn't know about the invasion. His father didn't know about it. He and his friends would need to tell them. Admit that they had left the city. Take the chance that this was important information and that they would not be punished.

As the boys approached, they heard water splashing in the fountain that contained the statue of the soldier Tremaine on his midnight black horse, Storm. They barely caught a glimpse of the fountain they often spent hours visiting, as they moved quickly into the marble hallways leading like rivers into the main stadium area.

They moved with expert knowledge of the structure, through the crowded passageways, until they reached the main area in front of the racetrack. Then they crossed the front row of seats until they were directly in front of the King's boxed section set behind white marble columns.

Climbing the steep marble stairs to the top of the stadium, the boys ignored shouts from friends. They weaved in and out of people clogging the steps in their endless pilgrimages to and from the food stands.

Finally, they reached the area owned by the King and his family. Keegan's mother, the Queen, waved her hand and yelled out to her son, "Hello, Keegan! Join us!"

Keegan and his friends passed between the marble columns and filled a long marble bench that his father had reserved for them. Keegan turned around to look at his father, then back toward the race, while he decided what to do.

His attention was momentarily captured by the chariot race. On another day, the race would have captured his heart and mind and filled his soul with dreams. Today, it simply distracted him by its sheer power and thunder.

There were five charioteers today. Five men, five horses, five chariots, five sets of brightly decorated costumes flying by like a splash of thunderous color in the wind. Onto each chariot was painted a unique shield design. The same design was tattooed on the chest and upper right arm of the man driving the vehicle.

Keegan and Wiley noticed that their favorite charioteer was in the race: Tyrone the Tempestuous. His shield, the boys thought, was magnificent: deep blue with the design of gathering storm clouds along the top and a black, whirling funnel cloud in the middle.

The chariots raced around the center island filled with thick, green grass. Brown dust, thrown up into the air by the horses' galloping hooves, floated over the island. Tyrone the Tempestuous, in his deep blue chariot trimmed with black lines, led the group. His horse, Rain Cloud, pounded out a thunderous war cry on the earthen track.

Close behind him raced Clayborne the Beast in his red chariot emblazoned with a picture of a fire-breathing dragon. His horse, Fire Breath, pounded out clouds of smoke around his strong black hoofs, as though setting the earth to smolder.

A short distance behind, Maxwell the Marvelous flew through the wind in his black chariot imprinted with white stars. His shield held half a moon, stars, and several planets. His horse, Golden Fury, stretched his legs, glistening in the sun, racing as though trying to reach the sunset itself by dinnertime.

A fairly significant distance behind the other three charioteers, came Radburn the Bear. His horse, Bear Claw, pulled a yellow chariot painted with the face of a bear on the back. The two sides displayed a black shield containing a white bear claw.

Behind Radburn and Bear Claw, raced Duncan the Daring and his horse, White Wind. A pure white stallion, White Wind had injured his leg earlier in the day and was having difficulty hauling the chariot as glistening and white in color as newly fallen snow. Small clouds of brown dust rose up and sprinkled onto the chariot, as though the earth had been turned upside down, dust falling from the sky on snow that had always existed.

Nevin pointed to the racetrack. "Look, Tyrone and Rain Cloud are winning!"

Wiley looked at Nevin. Had he forgotten about the invasion? Had he forgotten that their world as they knew it might end at any moment?

Wiley looked behind him at the King and then nudged Keegan. "Someone's whispering to your father."

"That's one of the palace guards."

Suddenly, the King stood up. Another palace guard spoke to the boys. "The King is leaving the stadium now. You boys must leave as well."

Keegan ventured a question, "Why?"

"I am not at liberty to tell you. Just come with me."

After the King and his family had reached the palace, trumpeters throughout the city blew loudly on their golden horns. Announcers shouted to the people, "Go home. The Festival of the Sun is ending early. Bad weather is on the way."

The people looked up at the Heavens. The sky looked perhaps slightly darker, but nothing of concern. Not wanting to take the chance of being caught in a bad storm, however, the people left their favorite entertainments. They filled the streets and moved, like fish swimming in the rivers, toward home.

CHAPTER 24

As King Reginauld and his family reached the palace gates, the King looked at his son and said, "Keegan, Wiley can stay overnight in your room tonight if you'd like." Then he looked at Keegan's other friends. "But, for all the rest of you boys, I will assign a guard to walk you home."

King Reginauld was tall and strong. He had thick, curly, golden hair that fell to his shoulders. On the top of his head rested a golden crown decorated with a myriad of dazzling jewels. His skin was rough, weatherworn, and etched with lines of worry. Wearing royal robes made of plush fabric hand-painted in patterns of purple, blue and gold, King Reginauld raised his right arm covered in a long, flowing sleeve. He then raised it higher as though trying to break free of a sleeve that had suddenly become too restrictive for the orders he had to give. With the pointer finger of his right hand, the King singled out, one by one, specific guards.

"Ramsey, you take Arthur home. Slade, you take Kingston home. Gaelan, go with Calder. Aldrich, take Nevin home." A flash of fear played across the King's deep blue eyes. "Nevin, where is Neil?"

"With my parents, Sir."

"Oh. Good. Well, let's move now, quickly! The crowds will be choking the streets in no time. Hurry! Keegan and Wiley, come with me into the palace."

The remaining guards surrounded the King, his family, and Wiley as they moved into the palace. Once inside, the King called a meeting of all high-ranking government officials and military officers. After the order had gone out, the King suggested strongly to Keegan that he and Wiley and go to his room and stay there until dinnertime.

Keegan was about to question his father on the need to stay in his bedroom; but thought better of it after considering the serious tone in his father's voice. Instead, he and Wiley dutifully followed the two guards assigned to escort them.

Once inside his bedroom, Keegan pushed the heavy wooden door shut. He briefly noted the picture hand-carved into his side of the door: the young boy dressed like a soldier, fighting a fire-breathing dragon with a sword, the sun shining brilliantly overhead with rays reaching down to earth, and a cave from which the dragon had stepped. The picture represented a myth famous within the city - a belief that there were dragons living deep within the caves outside the city gates, and a story that a boy would one day slay the beasts with the sword of a man. This story had been Keegan's favorite when he was a young boy.

Keegan turned around, leaned briefly against the door with his back, and then walked across the white marble floor.

Wiley had entered the room first. He noticed that both the heat and the glow crystals had been turned on. The walls and the floor felt warm to the touch due to heat crystals embedded deep within the marble. In addition, glow crystals in the shapes of stars set into the marble floor and walls twinkled as though descended from the night sky itself.

Keegan stepped onto the large turquoise rug in front of his bed, estimated the height of his mattress from the floor, and jumped with great force onto the thickly padded bed. From there, he whispered to Wiley, "In a little while, we'll sneak out and spy on the meeting. Come up here first. We can play toy soldiers and build walls with dice while we wait."

Wiley was happy to jump up onto the comfortable mattress and play soldiers; but he wasn't sure about spying on the King's meeting.

"Won't we get caught by the guards if we spy on the meeting?"

"No. I know a great hiding place. Trust me."

Wiley decided to forget about the meeting for awhile and to enjoy his playtime with Keegan. Keegan's room was easily ten times the size of his own room in the servants' quarters. The walls and floor were made from white marble heated by crystals. The windows ran along one side of the room. The windows and several sections of wall were covered in rich tapestries - midnight blue, hand-painted with a splash of white stars. The tapestries hung from golden rods decorated with silver half-moons on each end.

Lamps, lit by diamond glow crystals and topped by hand-painted shades, illuminated the living space of the room. Wiley's favorite lamp was a chandelier made from the carved wooden shapes of wild animals. Over the ring of wild animals hung a ring of diamond crystals cut into the shapes of stars.

The chandelier hung above Keegan's desk, a massive piece of wooden furniture. Each leg had been carved into the shape of a dragon whose fire breath supported the table.

On Keegan's desk, books were piled along the back edge, mainly his schoolbooks, but also books about dragons and caves. In the center of his desk marched an army of toy soldiers preceded by a toy King in a golden chariot.

Wiley picked up a handful of soldiers, horses and chariots and lined them up on a board Keegan had spread out earlier on his bed. The boys played for some time; then Keegan asked Wiley to be quiet. He listened closely to the sounds of the castle.

"I don't hear anything. The meeting has probably started. Let's go."

Wiley hesitated. "But isn't there a guard outside your door? Won't he stop us?"

Keegan looked at Wiley with surprise. "We're not leaving through my door!"

"What do you mean? How are we leaving?"

"I assumed you knew this. There are secret passageways throughout this castle, so that my family can escape if we're ever attacked. One passageway connects to my room."

"Really?" Wiley looked around the room. "Where?"

"Guess."

"I have no idea."

"I wish we had more time. I'd let you try to figure it out. But we've got to hurry. Come on. Follow me and do what I tell you to do. Don't question me right now. Just follow me."

Keegan jumped off his bed and landed on his feet. He then knelt down, looked under the bed, then crawled under.

"Come on, Wiley. I mean it. Follow me."

Wiley slid off the bed, landed on his knees, and then followed Keegan under the bed. Once Wiley joined him, Keegan pushed one of many star shapes in the floor. Wiley felt a rumbling, then saw a square marble slab drop lower than the rest of the floor and move sideways out of view.

Wiley stared at the opening. Keegan urged him to follow, "Come on. Hurry!"

Keegan slipped down into the opening. When his feet touched the floor inside the hole, his head was just below the floor to his bedroom. He walked ahead in the passageway in order to give Wiley room to jump down. Once Wiley entered the passageway, Keegan pressed a glowing turquoise button on the wall. The trap door slid shut and glow stars sprang to life, suddenly illuminating the dark tunnel.

Wiley felt both nervous and exhilarated. The experience felt a bit like walking through the heavens at night.

Keegan navigated his way through the winding passageway with Wiley close behind him. Suddenly he stopped next to another turquoise button.

"We're going back up now."

"Where are we?"

"You'll see."

As Keegan pressed the turquoise button, a marble slab descended a short distance from the floor above and slid sideways to the right. Keegan found a small step stool within an alcove in the tunnel wall, stepped on it, and hoisted himself up out of the tunnel. Next, Wiley used the step stool the same way.

Once the boys were completely out of the tunnel, Keegan pressed a star in the floor. The marble slab slid over, locked shut, and became once again a part of the floor.

Wiley looked around. "Where are we?"

"We're in a closet connected by a short hallway to the meeting room. Follow me."

Wiley followed Keegan. At the end of the hallway, Keegan slid behind a thick curtain hanging on a wall just inside the main room. Wiley followed him. The curtain hung down to the floor, providing safe protection for the boys. They listened attentively to the meeting.

Both boys recognized the King's deep, resounding voice. "So the mirror we provided worked?"

"Yes. Perfectly."

"Did the village people have any difficulty using it?"

"No. The ship burned up and sank."

"Now what about our men who were caught stealing gold from the mines during the Festival? Is the village taking any action against us?"

"I don't know. I would think they wouldn't want to risk angering us because they need our weapons and our support. But our truce has always been fragile. I would prepare our soldiers for war, just in case the invasion from outside stops and the village decides to attack us."

Keegan heard his father clear his throat. "I suppose you're right. Send out the order for the soldiers to prepare for possible battle. Warn them not to antagonize the villagers. As far as we know, the villagers won't attack. But we need to be prepared."

"I'm on my way."

"Well, then, let's adjourn this meeting. Tomorrow our citizens should resume their lives as normal. We'll tell them that we were wrong about bad weather approaching. They'll grumble at first about the Festival ending early; but then they'll get on with life as usual."

"And, Sir, what do you want us to tell your son?"

"Tell him that we were wrong about the weather. I'll tell his mother, the Queen, and his teachers that I want Keegan to go to the library tomorrow and read books about weather."

Keegan's face and body tensed. He grabbed Wiley by the hand and pulled him, under the draperies, back out into the hallway. The boys ran quickly down the hallway and dashed into the closet. Keegan dropped to his knees, pressed several incorrect stars, muttered under his breath, then pushed the right star. The marble slab dropped from the floor and slid to the side. First Keegan, then Wiley, jumped into the opening. Keegan quickly hit the turquoise button, then turned and raced down the tunnel. Wiley ran closely behind him.

When the boys reached the area under Keegan's room, Keegan hit the turquoise button, waited for the opening to form, and then hoisted himself back up into his room. Wiley followed suit. Keegan hit the star on his bedroom floor to close the opening, just as he and Wiley slid from under his bed.

They jumped onto Keegan's bed, and a guard opened the bedroom door.

"Your father has given orders for the both of you to come to dinner."

Out of breath, Keegan answered as briefly as possible, "We'll be there. Ummm … We just have to clean up my toys."

The guard shut the door and waited outside.

CHAPTER 25

As Calder approached his house with the guard, the front door opened. His grandmother, an elderly woman with graying hair, stepped outside.

"Calder, we were worried about you. Our neighbors mentioned that the Festival ended early due to approaching bad weather."

"That's what the crowd was told."

"Well, come on in. Your mother is making dinner for all of us."

Calder's grandmother stopped and looked at the guard who towered over her.

"I'm one of the King's guards. He instructed us to walk Keegan's friends home."

"That is so thoughtful! We're very lucky to have such a kind and generous King."

"Yes, we are. Have a good evening." With that, the guard turned and walked away through the twisting and winding labyrinth of streets that led back into the heart of the city and then on to the palace.

Calder's grandmother placed her arm around her grandson's shoulders. Bent over with age, she was only a slight bit taller than her eleven-year-old grandson.

"We had planned on eating at the Festival; but, when it was cancelled, your mother stopped at a market stand and purchased freshly cooked stew before the stands closed."

"Oh, I love that! From MacGillifin's?"

"That's the place. They had a stand at the Festival. And guess what we have for dessert."

"I have no idea."

"Sweet blueberry pie from the market stand of the O'Tackneys."

"Oh, I love their pies! Hurry! Let's go in the house."

Bursting with enthusiasm and suddenly realizing that he was very hungry, Calder entered the house shouting, "Mother, mother! I heard we're having stew and blueberry pie for dinner!"

Calder's father walked into the living room. "Quiet down, boy! We'll have a delicious meal, but all in good time. Have a seat in the kitchen. Your Aunt Melvina and Uncle Osgood are here."

"Oh."

Calder bowed his head and walked quietly into the kitchen. His Aunt Melvina was his father's sister. She was very strict, believing wholeheartedly, as Calder's father did, that children should be quiet and well-behaved. Her husband was inclined to agree with her, as they did not have children of their own and he did not care for noisy children when he visited relatives.

"Hello, Aunt Melvina. Hello, Uncle Osgood."

Calder's aunt and uncle who had been facing away from the kitchen entrance, talking with his mother as she warmed the dinner, turned suddenly around. Calder's uncle spoke first, "Hello, boy, how are you?"

"Fine, Sir. Very good, thank you."

Calder's aunt smiled. "You have very good manners, Calder. You'll grow up someday to be a fine businessman or politician."

Calder's face blushed almost bright enough to match his red hair. His freckles appeared to fade. "That's not what I want to be. I want to be an actor."

Rather than continue an ongoing family argument over his future job, Calder walked past his aunt and uncle and over to his mother cooking at the stove. She was heating the stew in a large copper pot. As she stirred the mixture, Calder leaned his hands on his mother's shoulder, bent closer to the stove and took a deep breath.

"That smells incredible! MacGillifin's! This completely makes up for the Festival closing early!"

Calder's mother turned toward her son with widened green eyes. "Really?"

Calder laughed suddenly, exposing the gap between his two front teeth. "No! But it will certainly make me feel better!"

Calder's aunt brushed her long, dark hair away from her face. She had blue-gray eyes, black hair, and full, red lips. She took great pride in having strong opinions and the courage to express them. Likewise, her husband took pride in having strong opinions and a willingness to share them. For the most part, Calder's aunt and uncle agreed on important issues. When they didn't, they had loud, heated arguments, even in public places.

Calder's uncle looked up with deeply penetrating blue eyes, rubbed his balding head, and challenged Calder's father to an inquiry. "So, why do you really think the Festival closed early?"

Calder's mother turned quickly away from the stove in order to answer the question first. She glanced briefly at Calder, then at his uncle, as though trying to tell him to curb his opinions in front of his nephew.

"It was closed due to bad weather …"

Calder's uncle interrupted his mother. He threw back his head and laughed, then stated, "The weather was beautiful! The best I've seen in a long time! It was not due to the weather."

Calder's grandmother, now sitting at the table, bowed her head. Waving her right hand in the air, she announced, "They told us that bad weather is on its way!"

"And how would they know what kind of weather is coming?"

Calder's grandmother shook her head. "I don't know. Maybe someone returned from sea and reported a storm out to sea."

"And who returned from sea? No one has returned from sea for days."

Calder's mother sighed. "Can we just enjoy dinner? Melvina, will you put out the plates?"

As Melvina walked over to the wooden cabinets next to the stove, Calder sat down at the table. His father sat down as well.

Shortly thereafter, everyone was seated at the long, wooden table with a steaming bronze plate of stew in front of them. To the right of each person, Calder's mother placed a bronze cup filled with water from the local spring. She then sat down herself.

"So, where did everyone go at the Festival today?"

Calder answered first, hoping that he would not be found out for sneaking to the mines. "I went to the chariot races."

Calder's uncle looked at him with glistening eyes. "You were at the races? Wasn't Tyrone the Tempestuous amazing?"

"Yes! And Rain Cloud! I wish I could have seen the end of the race!"

"You didn't see the end?"

"No. I was with Keegan. The King made us leave early, before the announcement about the Festival closing early."

Calder's father smiled at his son and then looked at his sister. "It's nice that Calder is friends with the King's son, don't you agree?"

Calder ate his stew quickly, as though racing to the finish line of blueberry pie. He thought that perhaps this was the best meal he had ever tasted. He wondered briefly what tomorrow morning would bring in terms of weather. Would there be bad weather, or not?

CHAPTER 26

After eating a fish dinner smothered in thick, spicy sauce, Nevin and Neil sat around the kitchen table with their parents, playing a game of Chariots. The game had been Neil's idea. After the family had removed their dishes from the table and his mother had cleaned the surface, Neil ran to his bedroom and returned with thc Chariots board game. He laid the decorated stone slab on the table, begging everyone to play.

His father had said that that was a great idea. Since the chariot races had been cancelled along with the rest of today's Festival, their family would carry on the tradition of chariot races on the day of the Festival of the Sun. With a smile on his face and his chest puffed up with pride, Neil ran back into his bedroom, and then returned with handfuls of small objects: two dice and seven miniature stone chariots.

"Pick a color!" Neil threw the chariots onto the table.

Neil's mother winced. "Careful, Neil, don't chip them!"

"Sorry. Well, pick a color, everyone!" After a moment of silence, Neil blurted out, "Wait! Me first! I want the blue one, like the chariot of Tyrone the Tempestuous!"

"That's fine. Here, take it." Nevin handed his younger brother the miniature chariot made of blue stone. "I'll take the red chariot."

Neil's eyes lit up with delight. "Like Clayborne the Beast!"

Nevin laughed. "I suppose so."

Neil's father chose the black chariot.

Neil jumped up and down. "Like Maxwell the Marvelous! Mother, what do you want?"

"I'll take the yellow one."

Both Neil and Nevin started laughing.

"What's wrong with that?"

"Yellow is Radburn the Bear!"

Neil's mother looked at him with furrowed eyebrows. "And what's wrong with that?"

Neil's father leaned toward his wife, smiled at his sons, and stated quietly, "Radburn the Bear was losing the race, along with Duncan the Daring whose horse, White Wind, had an injured leg."

"Oh, that's not good. What if I pick purple?"

Neil laughed at the suggestion. "There was no purple chariot in the race today!"

"Well, I'll take purple then. That way, you won't know if my chariot was winning or losing."

Neil looked at his mother with a puzzled expression.

"I just like purple. I'll take purple."

Chariots was a board game for young children. The board held a picture of a stadium racetrack divided into different color squares. The object was to roll the two dice, move your chariot game piece forward as many squares as the number indicated on the dice, and then follow the directions on the square on which your chariot landed. The first player to reach the finish line on the game board would win the game.

Neil's copy of the Chariots game was an especially nice one, given to him by his father. It was made of marble with inlaid stone squares making up the racetrack. The chariots were likewise made from different types of stone, and the dice were made from clear crystal with black circular markings.

Neil and Nevin's mother picked up the purple chariot from the table and handed the crystal dice to Neil. "Youngest first. Neil, you go first. Nevin, you go second."

Their father laughed. "Youngest first? I guess I'm last again!"

As Neil threw the dice onto the table, his father stood up and turned on the crystal glow lamps. A warm light flooded the room.

"Two! I got two!"

Nevin responded to his brother's outcry, "Two? That's good!"

"Yes!" Landing on a purple square with three gold dots and a black arrow pointing forward on the track, Neil then moved forward three more squares.

"I'm winning!"

Pretending to hit him, Nevin lightly tapped his brother on the head with an outstretched hand. "Of course you are! You're the only one who's moved so far!"

"Yes; but I feel lucky!"

Nevin threw the dice and rolled four. His square had a picture of a horse stable.

Neil leaned in toward the table on folded arms and smiled. "You have to skip a turn to feed your horse! I'm winning! I'm winning!"

Neil's mother ran her hand through her youngest son's hair. "Quiet down, Neil. The game is just beginning."

The game lasted until the boys' bedtime. In the end, Neil won. Before climbing into bed, he carefully tucked his game away in its special wooden box and placed it on a shelf in his room. Saying goodnight to Nevin, he added, "Next time you'll win, Nevin. Thanks for playing."

Nevin rubbed his brother's head. "You bet I'll win next time!"

CHAPTER 27

After returning home from the Festival, Kingston waited for his parents to return. He knew that his father would be one of the last people to leave the Festival, as the actors would need to clean and cover the open-air stage. His mother cooked for the actors and would need to pack up the food before returning home.

Kingston decided to go upstairs to his bedroom to wait. He turned on a crystal glow lamp next to the big, comfortable blue chair in his room and started to read his favorite book, The Boy from the Moon. In this book, a young boy came down to earth from the moon in order to teach a village that crystals as bright and shining as the moon existed within caves in the mountains next to their home.

Before long, the day caught up with Kingston, and he fell fast asleep under the light of a large crystal glow lamp.

CHAPTER 28

When the guard walked Arthur to his home, the boy thanked the guard and went inside. Hearing his mother moving around upstairs, Arthur decided not to yell out to her. Instead, he waited until he heard the guard walking away. Then he waited a few moments longer and slowly opened the front door. The guard was gone!

Quietly shutting the door behind him, Arthur walked down the street toward the back gate of the city. He wanted to find out if anyone was still at the mine, or if anything more was happening in the harbor of The Village by the Sea. He also wanted to find out if any people from his own city, The City of the Golden Sun, were out and about.

Most of the day, Arthur had spied on the men in the mine. He had watched, as men from his own city had removed gold from the section of mine owned by citizens of The Village by the Sea. He had watched, in nervous puzzlement, as men from his city had emerged from the earth, over and over again, to add piles of glistening rock to an ever-growing heap.

After bringing his friends to the gold mine, Arthur had witnessed a significant turn in events. The flash of light; the ship exploding in the harbor. What was going on?

He had to know.

When Arthur reached the back gate, he saw that guards were now patrolling the area. He could not leave the city.

Fearing that he would be caught, Arthur turned around and, disappointed, walked back home. As day turned into dusk, Arthur realized that the street glow lamps had not turned on. Soon the city would be plunged into darkness.

CHAPTER 29

The City of the Golden Sun and The Village by the Sea were both awakened by the singing of birds.

People stepped outside and looked up at the sky. There was great disappointment in the city that the weather was beautiful and the birds melodious. The Festival had been cut short for nothing.

In order to deal with their disappointment, many people decided to fill the day with work, to make up for the work time they had missed the previous day.

Wiley asked permission to go to the library to read about the history of the Festival of the Sun. Kingston and Calder decided to go to the library in order to find books for research reports they had been assigned about ships. Keegan had been instructed to find books about weather.

Neil and Nevin's mother decided to take her sons to the library in order to find new fiction books to read.

When Arthur entered the library in order to search for documents about the gold mines and anything written about mirror weapons, he found his friends already there, hard at work paging through books.

As the boys settled down to work, the sound of pounding horse hooves shook the library door. The adults instructed the boys to stay in the library.

Obeying their curiosity rather than the orders from the adults, the children poured out the front door one by one.

Noticing that soldiers on horseback were pointing up at the sky and shouting, everyone, children and adults alike, looked up at the sky. A large, glowing fireball with a hot, luminescent tail had fallen from the heavens and was rapidly making its way toward earth.

One soldier shouted over the clamor of horses' hooves, "It's punishment! It's punishment!"

Assuming that the soldier meant punishment from The Village by the Sea for stealing their gold, Arthur ran from one of his friends to another, urging them back into the library.

CHAPTER 30

The boys huddled in a corner of the library as the meteor hit. The sound exploded and was deafening. The meteor crashed, like the moon itself, into earth. The island buckled. Earthquakes split the ground. Then the rains fell – long, drenching, hypnotic rains. The sky blackened deep as night. The golden sun disappeared. Far away, just outside the city, the mountains of gold fell back into the earth.

Five handfuls of people fled to the caves in the mountains, either because they believed that they might be saved when a boy came to slay the fire-breathing dragons, or simply because they hoped to climb above the rising water.

The boys in the library fell fast asleep on the second day of the hypnotic rain.

They awoke to the sound of chirping dolphins. The door to the library flew open into what appeared to be the ocean. No water came in. Outside the door was a wall of water. A liquid wall filled with three dolphins, a white whale, and floating seaweed.

Elden communicated with the boys, "Come on, boys. Your time is up here. You have reconnected with your people, and you have learned what you need to know. Now, follow me."

Without questioning, as though they had rehearsed this scene a thousand times, Keegan and Arthur climbed onto Beluga's snow-white back. Nevin and Neil climbed onto Colt's back; and Kingston and Calder climbed onto Gladwin's back. With his friends safely protected within the ocean depths, Wiley climbed onto Elden. He took a moment to wrap his arms around Elden's wide neck in an affectionate embrace.

"I knew you'd come! I knew you would!"

"You remembered me?"

Wiley thought for a moment, "When the floods came, I remembered you. Perhaps the water reminded me of the ocean."

Elden communicated to all of the boys: "You will now remember me always. You will remember Beluga, Colt, and Gladwin as well." Elden paused, "And you will remember the ancient times, The City of the Golden Sun and The Village by the Sea. Wiley, even you will remember your travels back in time."

Wiley was about to answer when suddenly a scene materialized within the ocean depths. It was Wiley himself as he slayed the Fire Beast. The Beast was at least fifteen times the height of a house. It had the body of a dragon and a long, bending neck that resembled a snake. As it roared with incredible rage, moving its head from side to side, it flooded the water with fire.

Riding on Beluga's back, holding tightly onto the golden sword, Wiley sped toward the Beast. The water boiled. The fire reflected off the sword in explosions of red and orange and yellow.

As the Beast waved its long, snaking head from side to side, Wiley came up under its belly and stabbed its stomach with the glittering sword. Purple blood poured from the Beast and dyed the water. The Beast roared and growled and spit fire, as he shook his head furiously in rage. He stamped his feet, scraped his sharp claws along the ocean floor, and sent clouds of sandy smoke into the boiling purple water.

Wiley watched with wide, unblinking eyes, as he saw himself clutching the sword tighter and driving it into the neck of the Beast. He watched silently as the Beast flung him off in a desperate attempt to escape the searing pain. The ocean floor shook, opened, and swallowed the Beast whole. Only a purple stain remained.

As Wiley watched, the image of himself swam over to the purple stain and rubbed his hands through the sand. Suddenly, all of the darkened, purple grains of sand glittered, swirled over the spot where the Beast had been slain, and disappeared into the depths of the ocean.

Wiley clutched tightly onto Elden's back fin. His heart pounded in his chest. "What was that, Elden?"

"That was the effect of time warp. Look at where you are."

Wiley and the boys turned and looked around. In the returned darkness of the ocean floor, they saw the gate that had led in happier times to The City of the Golden Sun. They looked closely at the thin, golden bars, decorated with thousands of multi-colored gemstones.

Through his mind, Keegan read out loud to the other boys, the dolphins, and Beluga: " Drink deeply by land or sea. Earth comes only once."

Elden explained, "When you warp time, sometimes parts of it rebound - perhaps the most important parts, the incidents that shape our lives and all of time afterwards. I don't know. I just know that I have seen it before, and that the events have always been meaningful." Elden paused, as though trying to find the right words. "Wiley, do you remember the myth in The City of the Golden Sun that a boy will someday fight a dragon outside the city limits?"

"Yes."

"You are that boy. You came back through time. You slew the Beast. You have set a new generation free."

Wiley and his friends absorbed this information slowly and with reluctance. It takes time for myth to catch up with reality in the human brain; and the boys were very young and very new at this.

As they traveled through the ocean, from the lowest depths up to Wiley's island, the boys also moved in their minds from ancient times up to Wiley's present.

As they observed the colors of the sea – lazy green turtles, startlingly bright red fish, a shark surrounded by a wall of glittering silver fish, and so much more – the boys heard now and then the resounding songs of the great humpback whales.

The boys found this strangely comforting, this suddenly too familiar liquid world as they contemplated their future mission. It was up to them to bring the ancient ways to Wiley's struggling, impoverished island.

Sensing their concern, Elden reminded the boys, "Remember this: 'Drink deeply by land or sea. Earth comes only once.' Be thankful for what you have. You all have a second chance."

Wiley thought about this. As he wrestled to unwrap Elden's meaning, a sea turtle swam lazily past, staring at the boys on the backs of sea creatures. The boys stared back.

All would be fine. The songs of the humpback whales told them so. Life would go on. Time could bend and twist and warp; but life would rise up and greet the dawn, whether the sun rose in ancient times or in Wiley's time.

Bathed in liquid, the boys traveled through time to meet their future. The humpback whales repeated their ancient songs. The songs told of a time when a golden sword would unite past and present, present and future. The songs told of a day when the ancient city would rise again.

The boys knew none of this. The songs simply enlivened the ocean and comforted the boys on their long journey home.

ABOUT THE COVER ARTIST

Ardy M. Scott always considered herself a jack-of-all-trades and master of a few. To date she is an accomplished writer of new age fantasy with two books published and two more in the works. She currently runs two businesses from her home: FantaSeeWorks Graphics & Designs with her partners Michael in Canada and her husband Ken, and Fantasy In Wood (wood sculpting). More, she is also a freelance artist, doing original art, cover artwork and illustrations for herself, various publishers and independent authors.

Although born a Canadian, Ardy currently resides in North Queensland, Australia with her Aussie husband Ken. Formerly of Vancouver, BC, she acquired degrees in Criminology and Psychology from the University of Fraser Valley. She is a qualified Emergency Medical Technician (ambulance attendant) having attained her certification from Southern Alberta Institute of Technology; worked part-time for Dolphin Investigations as a Private Investigator; and ran a Parent Counselor home for The Ministry For Children and Families.

Ardy is currently the Associate Publisher of Futures Mysterious Anthology Magazine and Managing Editor for Twilight Times Books.

ABOUT THE AUTHOR

Marilyn Peake grew up in a small town in Pennsylvania, spending many afternoons climbing trees and exploring the woods in her three-acre backyard. Always interested in writing, she experimented as a young child with writing short stories. In high school, she wrote newspaper articles for two local newspapers.

In college, the author graduated with a Bachelor of Arts in Psychology. She later obtained a Master of Arts in Clinical Psychology. She has worked as both a Social Worker and Staff Psychologist in a variety of settings. In 1985, she completed a Masters Thesis, later presenting her research data at a meeting of the Eastern Psychological Association.

At the present time, the author lives in Virginia with her husband and two children. Her hobbies include photography and traveling. She has traveled with her family to Mexico, Hawaii, and the Caribbean islands. In Mexico, the author photographed fish while snorkeling underwater.

The Fisherman's Son is the author's first children's novel. The City of the Golden Sun is the sequel.

Printed in the United States
20995LVS00007B/91

9 781418 410575